INFINITE MOON

/ / / /

J.R. RAIN

&

MATTHEW S. COX

THE VAMPIRE FOR HIRE SERIES

Moon Dance
Vampire Moon
American Vampire
Moon Child
Christmas Moon
Vampire Dawn
Vampire Games
Moon Island
Moon River
Vampire Sun
Moon Dragon
Moon Shadow
Vampire Fire
Midnight Moon
Moon Angel
Vampire Sire
Moon Master
Dead Moon
Lost Moon
Vampire Destiny
Infinite Moon

Published by
Crop Circle Books
212 Third Crater, Moon

Copyright © 2020 by J.R. Rain

All rights reserved.

Printed in the United States of America.

ISBN: 9798654550712

Chapter One
On the Fly

Frantic emotions make it difficult to think.

My entire vampiric life thus far feels as though it's been leading up to this point: a confrontation with Elizabeth. The emotional strain of constant vigilance, worrying what she'd do and when she'd do it has eclipsed my memories of mortality to the point they're more like a dream than anything I've ever lived through.

Ever since she'd escaped from me, I've expected she'd do *something* bad. The only questions I had were 'when, and how many are going to die?' To be fair, my assumptions proved a bit off. We'd all been bracing for her attacking us: meaning my family, possibly Kingsley and Allison as well. Turns out, she didn't really care about us one way or the other.

Perhaps a little hubris came into play, but the

woman *did* have me convinced for quite a while the only thing standing between her and the ruination of the world as we know it was me. Yeah, also a lie. Not exactly sure what benefit it provided Elizabeth other than getting me to resist her taking over my psyche entirely. Maybe a host 'letting them out' fuses dark master and host together in a way where she couldn't simply leave whenever she wanted to, so she had to trick me into doing everything I could to keep her in a metaphorical pit in my head. I suppose it would also imply a dark master can't help themselves but attempt to infiltrate their host's psyche.

Or I could be completely wrong.

Elizabeth adores messing with people and causing emotional pain. She might have only been mocking me for being proud of my becoming a federal agent, thinking I made a difference for good in the world. I confess to a little pride, but no one goes to HUD for glory. Eight out of ten people probably don't even know the agency exists. Hollywood is riddled with movies starring fictional FBI agents or CIA agents. Can't say I've seen even one film about a Housing and Urban Development agent.

Whatever.

Point is, Elizabeth separated herself from me awhile back, and ever since, we knew she gathered her strength for something big. I'd mistakenly assumed she planned to raise an army of immortals and conquer the world. Believe it or not, ancient mysticism doesn't have a big advantage over modern weapons. Vampires are tough, but if Elizabeth took them public and tried to overwhelm entire nations, big bombs, tanks, military aircraft, and so on would get involved.

She'd probably set off nuclear war—sorta like that guy in Florida who burned down his entire house trying to get rid of a cockroach.

No, the *only* way a creature like her could take over this world would be subtle manipulation of prominent leaders behind the scenes. And while such a plan is completely within her powers, she doesn't want to be subtle anymore. This crazy bitch wants to be an empress, queen, or some such thing like a goddess on earth. Sorry, Liz. You might be fast, but you can't outrun a hellfire missile from a Predator drone. Can't mind control one of those either. Blow a vampire into tiny enough chunks, especially with fire involved, and it *might* be game over. Though, I have a feeling she would drift off somewhere and regenerate a new body.

I got a peek at her frustration when Izeth the ninth-dimensional being nearly exploded. Guess when you've been planning something for centuries, an unexpected failure is exceptionally infuriating. Damn her for fooling me again. Sitting there having tea and talking came too close to making me think of her as an actual somewhat-human being with functioning emotions and depth of personality.

Looking back on it, I'm sure she had no intention of releasing the creators she abducted alive. If her plan worked, she'd have needed them to essentially prop up the world they made. Without getting the creators' work out there into the sphere of public awareness, it would have ceased to exist without them. Her entire reality would only have existed by virtue of the creators mentally living in the world they made. As soon as they died, bye-bye everything. She probably would've turned them into vampires, maybe brought them into the world with her so they had the motivation of oblivion keeping them working on it for eternity.

Anyway, back to my whirling emotions. Not only do I have the worry, fear, and adrenaline rush that comes with the manifestation of my biggest anxiety of the past few years coming to fruition (the war between Elizabeth's dark masters and everyone else), I also get to freak out over bringing my damn kids with me.

This is elevating 'take your kids to work day' a bit too far.

Tammy emits a noise... part sigh, part giggle.

She's scared, but dealing with it. Can't blame her at all. Of everyone here, she's the closest to a normal person. Even Allison can defend herself with magic to a point. Granted, one of those ascendant dark masters would easily kill her before she even knew an attack was coming. They're ridiculously fast, though Kingsley probably has the reflexes, at least in wolf form, to deal with them. He's also far tougher than an average human, so a hit or two won't be instant death. Any ascendant who bites Kingsley is in for a rude awakening. He bites back, and his fangs are *way* bigger.

Even Anthony, at least if he shifts into the Fire Warrior, could probably protect himself against ascendant dark masters. The big burning guy isn't terribly fast—albeit he *is* much faster than a person would expect from looking at him—but my son has impressive dexterity. Probably from working out with Jacky and boxing. He'd have a better chance of catching an ascendant by the throat or punching them in the face than diving out of the way.

Point being, Tammy is an ordinary human girl with ridiculous telepathy, who doesn't belong anywhere near a fight with supernatural beings strong enough to throw cars. Fortunately, she's got long range skills. She doesn't have to be close to the dangerous parts to read minds.

Anthony thinks of her like 'command and control' from one of his video games. She's our radar and communications system, so to speak. My daughter can allow us to all basically communicate (through her) as though we had radios. Plus, she can sense the presence of sentient minds trying to sneak up on us and give us warning. Most importantly, however, she can mask us from Elizabeth's ability to detect our presence.

That reason, more than any other, is why she insisted on going with us.

Another source of my crazy emotions is how rapidly everything is moving. Elizabeth and her people took a magical gateway straight from

Barrow, Alaska to somewhere in Venezuela. She's planning to invade another dimension, but not one above ours. Going laterally prevents certain annoying issues like eventual complete disintegration—always a plus.

Her plan is to invade an alternate version of Earth containing a far more primitive civilization so she doesn't need to worry about laser-guided smart bombs or nukes. It's also supposedly 'more magical' than what I think of as our 'normal' world. I've got no idea exactly what it means to be more magical… anywhere from dragons flying around like sparrows to people like Allison making up a significant portion of the population. Good chance, magic in the dimension Elizabeth has targeted isn't something people try to keep hidden and/or don't believe in.

In her ascendant form, she has access to the full range of the abilities she had in her mortal life plus all the perks of immortality. I'm also not sure if we should consider ourselves lucky Elizabeth's forte is ritual blood magic. This means, she's not going to do—I'm guessing—the 'stand there and throw fireballs' thing like Allison. Oh, wait. She tried to impale me on an earthen spire.

Yeah, I'm anxious as hell because everyone is rushing, trying to stop Elizabeth from opening a portal to the other dimension. It would've been one thing to let her rule a world the creators made up for her, since everyone in it never would have existed otherwise. However, I can't just sit idly by while she spreads pain and misery over already-existing actual people. Just because they live in an alternate world doesn't make them less than real.

Worse, Tammy saw a vision of men tied to trees in a ritualistic manner, their chests bare and painted in arcane markings. Since they all wore olive drab pants, she thinks they might be soldiers. Kingsley suggested the idea of criminal gangs, mercenaries, or rebels as well, all of whom might be wearing 'military type' uniforms. Since, according to him, all sorts of 'bad guys' are down there.

Great.

It's like having to run through a swarm of wasps to get to the fire in the corner of a backyard so we can put it out.

Max has a private jet, much to my surprise. He's gathered up all the Light Warriors in close proximity who aren't either children-in-training or too old to help. They'd been preparing to meet us up in Barrow, but changed plans when I updated them on her sudden relocation.

Once Kingsley arrived at my house, I teleported us all to LAX.

Speaking of teleportation, I almost used Google Earth to jump us straight to Venezuela, but allowed Kingsley and Allison to talk me out of it. Allison worried Elizabeth would expect this and might have put up a temporary magical trap. The last thing I'd need is to try teleporting down there and being forcibly redirected into the heart of, say, a volcano or some such thing… or potentially across dimensions. Kingsley thought teleportation risked us leaping into an ambush of a more mundane type, and also believed the people Tammy saw about to be sacrificed had already been killed by now.

He has a point. It doesn't seem like ritualists would tie their victims to trees days in advance.

It also bothers me Anthony is so calm about everything. To see him sitting in his seat on Max's plane with his PlayStation portable, you'd think we were on another European vacation trip… or popping down to Venezuela to visit Aunt Elizabeth for a nice family gathering.

There's a fine line between confidence and recklessness, and I don't really like where an almost-sixteen-year-old boy puts that line. I set the bar a little higher.

Ever since Tammy found Elizabeth, and the woman stared right back at her, she's been quiet and more than a little freaked out. Don't think she's let go of my hand for a full five minutes ever since. I'm sure if she was still as small as a four-year-old, she'd be curled up in my lap. As it is, we're about the same size now. My daughter is still a bit skinnier than me, but she's a teenager. That'll change in a few years.

Tammy pokes me in the side, managing a nervous laugh.

I say, "Hey, any forty-seven-year-old who can still fit in the same clothes she wore in college is happier about that than if she won the damn lottery."

"Are you saying you won the lottery?" asks Tammy.

I shrug. "Some days, hell yes. Other days, not so much."

I think about Mary Lou, but not in an insulting way. She's normal. She's what I'd have looked like at fifty-three. No, ML isn't fat. She's *normal.* Which… Hollywood morons would call fat. Having three kids and a fondness for wine has certain effects on the body.

To distract my daughter, I end up rambling about my sister's kids on the flight south. Ruby Grace is a noodle. She's going to be sixteen in April, but she looks like a tall twelve-year-old. The girl spends so much time reading, studying, and doing academic stuff, she barely eats. Of course, she's probably going to skip senior year of high school (due to graduating early) and enroll in college. Ellie Mae is twenty and could probably have made a go of it as a model. Billy Joe has turned into quite the athletic young man. He's eighteen, very handsome, and likes to lift weights. He's no Hulk, but he turns the ladies' heads.

We lament the ravages of time on the human body for a little while. Tammy doesn't mind the idea of growing old. Considering we're heading to Venezuela to get in Elizabeth's way, she's mostly worrying about *not* having the chance to get old.

***

When we're thirty minutes from Venezuelan airspace, Tammy takes off her faerie amulet and begins to concentrate on cloaking us mentally from any vampires out there who might be able to detect our presence. Unfortunately for her, it leaves her vulnerable and unaware of her surroundings. Sort of like a meditating monk, only she has enough faculty left to zombie shamble around if someone is there to help steer.

Max walks up and down the aisle, handing out small booklets.

"What's this?" I ask, taking one.

"Enchanted passport." He smiles. "Looks blank to you, but if you hand it to someone expecting to see a passport, it will appear as one in their mind. Also, it will fog their judgment and compel them to let you by with minimal questions."

"Oh. Neat. Thanks."

He nods, hands me one for Tammy, and keeps going.

After the plane lands at Simón Bolívar International Airport in Caracas, I help my daughter out of her seat, pull her arm around my shoulders, and basically carry her. She's acting more messed up now than the night I found her 'pass-out drunk' at a party.

At the customs area, one agent keeps giving her suspicious looks. By the time our turn in line comes, he appears ready to either call for an ambulance or a cop.

Anthony pats her on the shoulder and manages a

passable, "My sister's special needs" in Spanish.

Tammy snarls in the back of my mind.

"She's gonna whack you with a pillow for that when this is over," I mutter.

"I know." He smiles, handing the guy his fake passport. "She's cussing me out already, though I could barely hear her."

"Well, she's kinda distracted right now."

Surreal is watching a Venezuelan official looking at a tiny blank book, nodding, stamping it, and handing it back to my son as though nothing strange went on. Once the kids, Kingsley, Allison, and I are done with the checkpoint, we walk a short distance down the big corridor and stand in a group with some of Max's people. While waiting for the rest to bluff their way past the customs agents, I take advantage of being in a crowded place. There are so many people here it's easy for me to feed.

Eventually, the remaining Light Warriors are past the security station. Like some kind of strange tour group, we move en masse to the foyer near the airport's main entrance. None of us have brought much in the way of luggage, spare clothes, or even toiletries. It's all rushed and last-minute. Some of Max's people have small bags, though they all look like they ran out the door in whatever they had on in the moment.

Max approaches us, forming a circle with me, Kingsley, and Allison. Anthony is a little behind me on the right, holding Tammy up while she focuses on hiding us from Elizabeth or anyone loyal to her.

"Any idea where the hell we're supposed to be going from here?" asks Kingsley.

"Tam can't search for her without giving us away." Anthony adjusts his grip on her. He can't pull her arm across his shoulders like I did, or she'd be off the ground.

"Should we get a hotel?" asks Allison. "Or just find some place to hang out?"

Max taps a finger to his chin. "Yes, a hotel would make the most sense."

I nod at the group. "That works. You guys go make whatever preparation you need at a hotel. I can go try to see if anyone in the city knows anything."

Mom, don't get too far away, says Tammy in my mind. *Past five miles, I can't hide you.*

Max, Kingsley, Allison, and Anthony nod simultaneously, all hearing her 'group' broadcast.

"Well, I highly doubt she's in Caracas," says Kingsley. "Far too many people, not enough privacy."

"Indeed." Max nods. "Though she needs a major ley line nexus. We've discovered six signi-ficant intersections in Venezuela, three of which are rumored to be quite powerful. The problem is, they're hundreds of miles apart and all in the jungle. Sadly, I believe the presence of modern technology and so many people who no longer respect mystical traditions have eroded the lines in the bigger cities. We will likely need to travel south into the jungle. Tammy's vision did show an area of lush vegeta-tion.

However, we're looking at an area encompas-sing hundreds of square miles."

"Someone in town here has to have seen something I can pluck out of their heads," I say.

"Remember, Ma," says Anthony, "that ninth-dimensional alien thing made a gateway straight to the ley line nexus," says Anthony. "They didn't exactly go through customs."

"Good point." I fold my arms, thinking.

"Doubt she's within a hundred miles of Cara-cas." Kingsley sniffs the air.

I reluctantly accept it will be useless to roam around the city randomly reading minds. "Well, crap."

Allison raises both eyebrows. "I could try the ol' crystal ball again."

"Excellent idea." Max smiles, hanging up his cell phone. "I've made arrangements at a nearby hotel for us."

"Lead the way." I gesture at the airport exit. "We don't have a ton of time."

Chapter Two
Dead Man Talking

My son amuses himself by making a game out of minding his sister.

He's acting as if she's a really lifelike stuffed animal he can pose on chairs, or, once in the hotel room, see how many pillows he can stack on top of her head. She's too out of it from concentration on masking us to offer any protest, though I have a feeling she will pay him back somehow, as soon as doing so won't kill us all.

Max had arranged rooms for us in a decent hotel. What passes for 'nice' down here is roughly on par with a giant Best Western. According to Kingsley, there's a major jump from 'meh' to astoundingly expensive, sort of like having a crumbling hotel across the street from the Ritz Carlton. This place isn't exactly falling apart around us, but five star it ain't.

I sit with Allison on the floor along with two of Max's people, Yasmeen and Olivia, both mystics gifted with scrying. Yasmeen looks about Tammy's age. The girl has a bit of an accent, though I can't tell which part of the Middle East she came from. Olivia's right around thirty and never outgrew the goth phase. Jet black hair, pale skin, and pigtails are a bit weird to me on a woman her age, but, hey. Whatever.

Allison sets up her crystal ball (she brought her supplies since she had them right there at my house). The four of us hold hands and start trying to get a read on where Elizabeth is. While we do this, Kingsley and Max make arrangements for dinner. Anthony keeps an eye on his sister.

An hour later, the guys walk in carrying aluminum trays of food. Mostly barbecued chicken, pork, and sausage over rice. Predictably, Kingsley eats a ridiculous amount. Anthony does quite a bit of damage, too. Tammy's got enough function to chew, but I have to feed her.

Having had no luck thus far, we take a break to eat, then resume.

A few minutes after the four of us focus magical energy into the crystal ball, a transparent man wearing a plain dark green military uniform phases into the room through the wall. Ordinarily, a ghost appearing wouldn't startle me into jumping, but this guy's been slashed open from throat to belly. I'm not jumping at the presence of a ghost, but the shocking amount of gore. At first glance, one might mistake the wound for the result of pissing off a lion, but the slashes run too deep and have sliced his bones, too. Something with beyond-human strength and claws far sharper than nature intended anything to have killed him.

My claws could make a similar wound, though perhaps slightly shallower.

Yeah, this guy most likely died at the hands one of Elizabeth's ascendant dark masters.

"We have a visitor," I say.

Allison, Yasmeen, and Olivia look at me. I point. The three of them glance toward the spirit, but only Allison reacts—by wincing like she just saw someone stub their toe.

"What is it?" asks Yasmeen.

"Ghost," I say.

"I'm going to try talking to him," says Allison.

"In Spanish?"

"Yeah. Hang on."

She does just that, introducing herself. This is followed by another sentence or two that I can't understand. Allison translates for us quickly. "I asked if he's here as a result of our opening ourselves to the spirit world or if he's just a curious local haunt."

The man speaks back in Spanish, far too rapidly for me to make sense of other than picking out his name, Jose Ureña, and something about monsters killing him. Via my mind link with Allison—which is easier to follow than having her translate—I pick up that he'd been a soldier of the Venezuelan government who was part of a group defending a 'cultural heritage site' from looters, criminal gangs, drug traffickers, and rebels. Jose describes 'tall, soulless monsters' coming out of nowhere in the middle of the night and slaughtering everyone in sight, including him.

According to Jose, Elizabeth and her army have taken up residence at an ancient Incan site deep in a region known as *El Caura.* Only one road, a dirt trail, leads anywhere near it, and still requires a two-hour hike to reach her camp. The closest city of any respectable size is called Ciudad Bolivar. He suggests we go there first and speak to a guy named Matias Reyes. The man runs a small mercenary outfit that sometimes does questionable things, but generally hires out to rich foreigners looking for 'jungle adventures.'

Reyes' group can lead us to the site he calls *Kancha Huanca.* Jose also tells Allison we will need an armed escort to have any chance of reaching the place alive, though we both initially sorta chuckle internally at the suggestion, since myself, Allison, Kingsley and Anthony as the Fire Warrior could probably hold our own. That said, the Light Warriors Max brought along are all ordinary people with magical abilities, most of which are designed to help them combat supernatural creatures and demons. Against ordinary humans and combat rifles, they probably *do* need a little help. At least having armed mercenaries escorting us would provide some cover. Hostile parties would focus on shooting at them before firing on anyone who appeared unarmed—plenty of time for me and my merry band of misfits to do our thing.

Allison eventually translates everything Jose says so Max, Kingsley, and the others can follow along.

"Why do we need to bother with these mercenaries?" asks Kingsley. "Can't this ghost lead us to the temple?"

Allison relays the question in Spanish, then listens to the ghost's reply. "He's only here due to our spell. As soon as we end it, he's going to be dragged back to the site of his death."

"Give me a few minutes." Max pulls out his phone and spends a while tapping the screen. "Hmm. Doesn't seem to be an airport at Ciudad Bolivar. Should be able to hire a bus, though."

"It's a couple hundred miles and there isn't exactly a six-lane freeway through the jungle," says Kingsley. "Elizabeth's going to be long gone before we're anywhere near the place."

Max offers a placating smile. "My mother isn't going anywhere, my good man. Not yet, anyway. Opening inter-dimensional gateways takes time. At least a week. Many days, certainly. We should have plenty of time to reach her."

I hold a finger up. "Except she has a ninth-dimensional being helping her."

Most of the color drains out of Max's cheeks. "I see. Then make that a day or two, tops. Still, we should have enough time. I recommend everyone turning in and get as much sleep as possible. I will make arrangements with the buses. We leave in the morning."

Allison thanks the ghost, who promptly vanishes.

It's a good thing I can replace sleep with extra feeding. No way am I going to be able to relax tonight.

Chapter Three
Mercenaries

The bus pulls up to the hotel less than half an hour after Max gets off the phone.

Nothing like money to make the world go around. On top of what the bus company wanted to charge for a short-notice trip to Ciudad Bolivar, Max promised the driver a $1,000 USD cash tip once we got there alive.

Waving a pile of money around is one way to motivate people to take a four-to-five hour ride on the spur of the moment. So, we all piled into a rickety old thing only slightly nicer than a school bus inside. Doesn't matter if the seats are crummy, almost everyone in our group catches a nap on the way.

Max takes a small bottle out of a boxy carrying case he's been lugging around and offers it to me. "Here, give this to Tammy."

It's about the size of one of those 'Five Hour Energy' shots, but dark blue. I look it over, one eyebrow up. "What is it?"

"She cannot eat, drink, or sleep while she remains focused on concealing us from Elizabeth. This elixir will satisfy her body's needs for twenty-four hours."

"Wow…" Allison whistles. "You could make a fortune selling that."

"I don't need to make a fortune." He smiles in an 'I already have one' sort of way. "And there would be no way to reveal this to the world without repercussions. Society is not ready for magic."

Tammy transmits a vague suggestion that if this potion works, she wants Max to give her some for hell week once she's in college. Hell week being the lead up to final exams when she'll be cramming.

I feed her the potion, which smells like blueberries.

Spanish music comes from a small speaker up by the driver's seat. I didn't get his name, but he's a short older guy in his early fifties with grey hair and a beard. Based on the animated conversation he had with Max upon his arrival at our hotel, I assume the driver agreed to Max's terms. That, and the somewhat dangerous pace the driver kept.

It irks me being unable to do anything but wait, but I have no choice. Going there alone is asking to get overwhelmed. Getting too far away from Tammy is also asking for things to go wrong. No telling what Elizabeth would do if she sensed me coming after her when she's this close to her goal. Maybe I'm thinking too much of myself. It's quite possible she'd sense me coming, simply roll her eyes, and laugh at little ol' me thinking I'm going to stop her. While I *am* fairly dangerous, no way do I think it possible for me to go in there and take on forty or fifty ascendant dark masters plus Elizabeth plus Izeth. No idea how much—if any—power the ninth-dimensional creature has in our world, but he has to be at least as deadly as any of the dark masters.

For that matter, I still haven't worked out exactly what to do once we get there, short of the most simplistic cavewoman approach: stab the bitch. Aside from having more telepathic power, and probably nastier magic, Elizabeth is physically similar to other ascendants. My Devil Killer has already proven itself capable of ending them for good. I start to wonder if Azrael gave me this sword because he knew I'd need it for her down the road, but decide it's an unintentional coincidence. The Angel of Death recruited me to be his protégé on Earth, tracking down demons. Neither Elizabeth nor I are significant enough to warrant actions 'in accordance with prophecy.'

This might all be as simple as flying in there on my angel wings and stabbing her. Sounds anticlimactic, but it just might work.

That she's also Max's one-time mother is another thing entirely.

Hard to kill a mother in front of her son.

Wow, this just got complicated.

With that thought, Max glances over at me and holds my gaze. No words pass between us, and no thoughts, but being like the second greatest telepath in the world, he knows what I'm thinking.

After a long moment, he finally nods.

He's given me permission to do what I need to do.

To do what he can't do... kill his own mother.

I think I'm going to be sick.

***

We arrive in Ciudad Bolivar a little after six in the morning local time.

As the bus rolls to a stop in front of another—much smaller—hotel, Max settles up with the driver, who plans to get a room and sleep. While the Light Warriors, Max, and my kids go into the hotel to clean up and get something to eat, Kingsley, Allison, and I begin searching for Matias Reyes. We don't have the time for doing things the traditional investigative way, so we cheat like hell.

Allie is better at Spanish, so she handles the bulk of the talking. I simply prod everyone she decides to approach with a mental command to 'answer her truthfully' in Spanish (a phrase Allison quickly taught me). Some aspects of vampiric mind control don't require knowing the victim's language. Basic, emotional prompts like 'run away in fear' or 'stand there staring into space like a simpleton while I bite you' operate on a primal level.

More nuanced commands, such as a desire to tell the truth, perform a specific task, and so on, require inserting the order via telepathy or actual speech. Needless to say, if the person doesn't understand what I'm saying, the command won't do anything but confuse them.

Hence, why I'm using the simple Spanish phrase.

A little more than an hour into our canvassing, a local cop points us to a part of town he doesn't think 'regular Americans' ought to go. Presumably, he means me and Kingsley. Again, we aren't worried about local tough guys, street gangs, or random mortal crazies, so we go there without hesitation.

Much to the astonishment of a cluster of rough-looking young guys hanging out in a cluster, Allison walks right up to them, as do I, not an ounce of worry on our faces. Kingsley's got an 'oh please start a fight' sort of smile. These guys *do* kinda look like they're considering bonking him over the head and having a little fun with the 'defenseless girls,' but Kingsley is freakin' huge. One weird thing about werewolves: they seem to get bigger the longer they live. At his present age, my man is at least on par with the upper third of WWE wrestlers.

Granted, a dude being huge doesn't necessarily mean he knows how to fight, but the look on Kingsley's face appears to be enough to keep these thugs from doing anything… yet. Allison starts asking them about Reyes. Once again, I slap them in the brain with a command to answer her truthfully.

One guy in a tank top and army pants points down the street and says something about a blue garage 'near all the wheel rims.' Satisfied, Allison thanks them and resumes walking. I give the men a strong craving to go have breakfast and forget they saw us. The—most likely—gang members head off in a group, talking about being hungry.

A few buildings down, we find a place somewhere between Sanford & Son's junkyard and an automotive service station from a post-apocalyptic world. Wheel rims and hubcaps of various sizes and condition adorn a chain link fence separating a huge front yard from the street we're on. We enter through the gate. On our way to the garage at the back of the property, we pass several cars, a few pickup trucks, and two enormous canvasback military style trucks parked on either side of the lot against painted concrete walls.

The garage is fairly large with two service bays next to an office area and small filling station. Most of the concrete is painted sky blue. Nine men are hanging out at the garage, three of whom are working on an older Land Rover up on a hydraulic jack. One of the dudes is only a little smaller than Kingsley. Most have handguns on belt holsters or AK-47s within arm's reach.

"Wow," mumbles Kingsley. "It's like the South American A-team… without the Hollywood budget. All that one dude needs is a cigar."

I snicker.

A thirtyish guy, one of the ones not doing

mechanic work, stands from the blue barrel he'd been sitting on and walks up to us. His expression is a mix of curiosity, annoyance, and amusement. His thoughts are in Spanish, though I catch enough to understand he's wondering who sent him a pair of hookers. He thinks Kingsley is our pimp. Not that we're dressed like whores or acting like it… he just can't think of any other possible explanation for a couple of women and a big guy to randomly walk into his place without a car in need of service.

I close my eyes and exhale out my nose. When I open them, the same guy's giving me a quizzical look. Now he's wondering if I'm some kind of Lara Croft crazy white chick who wants to go running around the jungle. He's thinking of Allie as my hired interpreter and, of course, Kingsley as our 'big strong dumb guy.'

Technically, Kingsley *is* our big strong guy, but he's not dumb.

"British or American?" asks the man, in English.

"American, but it has nothing to do with why we're here," I say. "We hear you can take us to *Kancha Huanca*."

He walks up to me, arms folded, taking me in. Guy's a lot taller than me, no surprise. I'm not exactly an Amazon, standing at five foot three. "Oh? Where did you hear that?"

"Know a guy named Jose Ureña?" asks Allison.

The man I assume to be Matias Reyes shoots her a dark look. "You must be mistaking me for someone else. It would be wise for you to be on your way and pretend you never came here."

Their big guy picks up a half-inch diameter metal rod, examines it, then looks right at Kingsley while bending it.

Kingsley chuckles, dusting his fingernails off on his shirt. As casual as can be, he walks over to the guy, looking at the rod.

Allison grabs my arm and whispers, "He's gonna rip the guy's face off. What do we do?"

"No, he isn't. Relax." I pat her on the hand.

Kingsley picks up a section of… is that a drive shaft? Gotta be from a truck. The thing's as fat as a pool noodle. He holds it up like a connoisseur examining an overpriced biscotti. The mechanics stop working and walk out of the garage to watch. Reyes and his guys all more or less laugh.

Kingsley turns the bar over in his hands. "Looks like scrap. Is it important?"

"It's scrap," says Reyes.

Kingsley smiles and grabs the other end of the shaft with his left hand. He waits a few seconds, letting Matias Reyes and his men chuckle a little more, then bends the drive shaft section in half, only a little effort showing on his face. Being hollow, it crimps, but still… the men all go silent, staring at him in bewildered awe.

I learn a few new Spanish swear words, as well.

Their big guy, his expression miffed, picks up the other half of the drive shaft—which is longer—and tries to bend it. His forehead goes red, veins rising. He emits a bunch of constipated grunts until nearly passing out from strain. Once it becomes apparent he can't, the men's demeanor changes. The thinly veiled hostility gives way to an 'all right, maybe you guys are okay' vibe. I swear as long as I live, I'll never understand men. What does bending metal rods have to do with anything?

"How do you know Ureña?" asks Reyes.

"We, um, contacted him yesterday," says Allison, referring to our conversation with his ghost. "Did you know him well? Were you close?"

"Were?" Reyes stares at her, anger seeping into his expression.

I get a read from his thoughts. Not family, but the two men have been friends since grade school. Damn. I speak gently, saying, "Jose was murdered a few days ago. We are hunting the people who did it."

"Murdered?" Reyes shouts. He's furious, but we're no longer the direct target of his rage.

The other guys whisper amongst themselves about 'that place' being cursed.

"Wait. Died a few days ago?" Reyes points at Allison. "But you just said you contacted him yesterday. What's going on?"

"I spoke with his *spirit*." Allison holds her hands up in a placating gesture. "I'm a psychic medium. He wants someone to avenge his death."

It's a crazy concept, and a lot for someone to accept who'd just been shooting the shit with his pals in a garage, so I give him a mental nudge to believe her words.

"Who killed him?" asks Reyes.

"Those who are at *Kancha Huanca*," I say.

"Dammit. Anywhere but there." He runs his hands through his hair.

"Matias, they will be leaving soon," I say. "We have to get there as soon as possible."

Reyes appears tempted to help, but hesitates due to an almost irrationally strong worry. The other men voice objections, protesting the 'curses' over the site.

"It's just that… my men will not go there," says Reyes, head bowed. "They believe the evil ones will destroy those who willingly go to such a cursed place."

Allison catches my eye. *Sam, show off your angel wings.*

Why?

It will convince them to help us.

But why would an angel need their help?

Don't worry about that now. They're all wearing crucifix necklaces and stuff. Lots of religious people down here. If they think you're an angel and have the ability to protect them from the evil in those ruins, they'll go.

Wow. Can I get in trouble for impersonating an angel?

She smirks. *You've met Azrael. You kinda* are *a deputy angel.*

Fair point. Okay, whatever. Not like we have time to sit around here arguing.

"You do not need to worry," I say in passable Spanish. "I will keep you safe from the curses."

The men stare at me, a whole lotta 'yeah sure, *chica*' in their eyes.

I summon my angel wings and spread them out to either side. At least this garage has a fully walled-in courtyard. Only these dudes can see me. "I've been sent to cleanse the evil in the place you call *Kancha Huanca*."

After a tiny bit of mental tweaking to stop them from wondering why an angel couldn't magically find this place without help, Matias Reyes and his men agree to take us on as clients. He quotes a rate of $18,000 for the escort, which goes up to $45,000 if they have to do any fighting.

"Fees won't be a problem," says Kingsley. "And once we reach *Kancha Huanca*, you and your men can leave us there. You won't need to get involved in any fighting at the site, and I suggest you don't. Bullets won't be effective against these guys, anyway."

The men exchange nervous whispers. Then gesture toward me. It appears they're putting their trust in the angel.

No pressure or anything.

I give Reyes and his men a prod of courage. "Meet us at the Bolivar Gran Hotel as soon as you're ready to leave. We're in a serious hurry."

Matias nods. "Twenty minutes."

Chapter Four
Welcome to the Jungle

Upon our return to the hotel, we brief the others on the situation.

Max decides to borrow the bus from our driver, leaving the still-sleeping man a note with a promise to return (or replace) the bus, and another $1,000 for 'the inconvenience.' He doesn't want to drag the guy into our mess. Kingsley ends up driving the bus, which I find hilarious. He's veritably spilling out of the seat.

We head southwest out of the city following two big Jeeps belonging to Reyes and his men, on a road named Nineteen. Not a whole lot out here in terms of civilization. Once we're away from the city limits, it's all undeveloped land with the occasional farm or tiny village. The second Jeep pulls into the oncoming lane and slows, letting us pass, before pulling in behind us.

An hour into the ride, Anthony begins tapping his foot and nodding along as if listening to music.

Tammy's weakened voice whispers in my head, *He's humming "Welcome to the Jungle." Since when does he listen to The Rolling Stones?*

I snicker. It's Guns 'N Roses, and I suspect it's your dad doing the humming.

Oh, you're right. Sorry, not thinking clearly.

On a side note... while my daughter doesn't hate Danny, she's still mad at him. Ever since she saw into my mind at how it made me feel when he took the kids and only let me have fifteen-minute phone calls with them—which he often denied—she's thought of him as an asshole. She didn't even care about me scolding her for using foul language. At the time, she'd been too little for her telepathic abilities to develop enough to penetrate Danny's mind, but even without it, she didn't believe his lies when he told the kids I 'was too busy' to talk to them. Exactly. The bastard told the kids *I* didn't want to talk to them on the phone when he flat out refused to let me.

Grr. I'm getting angry all over again thinking about it.

Eventually, we take a left off Route 19 and head almost due south over a tiny dirt path barely wide enough for a car, let alone a bus. It's only a few miles before we reach the start of literal jungle too thick to drive in.

Judging by the way the Light Warriors are all fidgeting and sweating, I'm glad I'm still wearing the hot/cold amulet Max gave me. Still feels like I'm hanging out in my house back home, a nice, comfortable seventy degrees.

Oddly, Anthony doesn't appear to mind the heat at all. Then again, he's probably so in tune with the Fire Warrior, he's inheriting some sort of sun-worshiper's tolerance for warm weather. The lead Jeep pulls off to the side of the dirt trail and stops. Kingsley parks the bus behind it. For some reason, I have an image of me throwing a spitball at the big oaf. Allison snickers.

Everyone gets out of their respective vehicles and assembles in a group.

Reyes explains we've gotten as close as vehicles can get. We're looking at approximately fifteen miles of hiking. "You guys should unload your provisions off the bus now."

"Already done." Max pats his carrying case.

About half the Light Warriors pat satchels and backpacks.

"You're kidding, right?" asks Matias.

His people all have large backpacks.

"There's a lot going on here you wouldn't believe," I say. "Trust me. They're fine."

One of the mercenaries speaks rapidly in Spanish, pointing toward Tammy, who's draped over Anthony's arms. Reyes translates. "He wants to know what's wrong with that girl."

"Oh, she's just stopping the evil spirits from sensing us," says Allison.

The guys seem to shrug it off, deciding not to

keep talking about 'that sort of thing.'

Reyes and a guy named Alejandro take point, leading the way into the jungle.

Within the hour, Allison curses, stops, and sits on the ground to pull her sneakers off. She conjures hiking boots directly onto her feet, then stands and resumes following us. Not a bad idea. Jungle hiking in sneakers isn't the smartest thing. But… I'm not going to worry about it. Any blisters I get will heal in minutes.

We continue on...

The average human walking speed is two miles per hour. I'm going to assume they base it on covering flat, unobstructed ground in a straight line. We are *not* walking over flat, unobstructed ground. It's going to take us between seven and ten hours—if not longer—to reach *Kancha Huanca.* Fingers crossed even Izeth can't whip up an interdimensional gateway in mere hours, or even a day or two.

Allison thinks given the circumstances, Elizabeth might be delayed by awaiting the arrival of all her loyal dark masters. After all, she'd likely need a small army to take over an existing world. Allison also thinks hopping to an existing lateral dimension is more of an instant one-shot thing. If so, they'd need to get everyone here all at once. She's also hopeful Izeth might not be as good at opening gateways as I assume since, as a ninth-dimensional being, he can freely jump between dimensions on his own as long as he's going downward from the ninth. He doesn't have to open gateways normally, because travel for him is as simple as wanting to go somewhere.

Here's hoping.

We walk until dark, dealing with streams, snakes, vines, mud, buzzing insects, and 'stuff that crawls.' Good thing Tammy's semiconscious or she'd be freaking out and miserable… like most of the Light Warriors. Facing off against demons is apparently easy peasy compared to dealing with flying insects so big they sound like helicopters going by.

Fortunately, whatever I am now, I'm not the least bit appealing to mosquitoes. Allison subtly *zaps* them every now and then, a tiny blue bolt of electricity crackling from her fingertip. Anthony doesn't appear bothered by the bugs, but when one lands on his sister, he promptly smacks it off her... sometimes a little harder than need be.

I'm gonna kill him, ma.

He's trying to help you.

He's helping a little too... vigorously.

I snicker.

Roughly ninety minutes after sunset, Reyes pauses, pointing at a small stone obelisk barely visible under a dense layer of vines. "We are almost there. This marker is a warning not to go on. Only those who revered the evil ones as gods can do so safely." He pauses, looking around. "Amazing."

"What's amazing?" I ask.

"We did not get shot at by looters or the military." He starts to chuckle, but trails off... clearly still worried.

"How much farther is it and where?" I ask.

Reyes points. "About a quarter mile."

"What are you thinking?" asks Max, approaching us.

I face him. "I'm thinking I'd like to sneak in close enough to get an idea of what we're dealing with."

"You're asking us to wait here while you go in alone?" Max raises both eyebrows.

"Like hell she's going in alone," says Kingsley, stepping next to me. "I'll be with her."

I sigh. I could probably move faster on my own, but it's pointless to argue with Kingsley when he gets protective of me.

Max nods. "All right. We'll wait for you."

We set out, and soon head past the 'death to all who go past this point' marker. Kingsley can be quiet if he has to, especially as a wolf. You know what's scarier than a ninja sneaking up on you out of seeming nowhere? When a 700-pound wolf sneaks up on you out of seeming nowhere.

When we're out of sight, Kingsley strips and shapeshifts into his wolf form. I stash his clothes under some vines and we head deeper into the jungle. Ten minutes later, the silhouette of a stepped ziggurat emerges from the foliage up ahead, but we don't get far before encountering a pair of human men in plain green uniforms, both carrying AK-47s. They appear to be Venezuelan Army soldiers. Their presence here, alive and apparently guarding the site, means one of two things. One, either the ghost lied and Elizabeth isn't here, or two, those men are mind-controlled puppets.

I don't want to kill them in either case. Unfortunately, we also can't allow them to make noise—especially firing their rifles. Only one truly viable option—avoiding them. We wait for the patrol to walk off to the left, then creep onward. Considering it's only the two of us and Kingsley is ridiculously quiet for his size, it's not too difficult to avoid notice. Don't imagine they're on guard for one or two people trying to sneak in. Anything in this place worth stealing is probably going to require trucks and heavy equipment to move. Most of the value here is in selling to museums, not so much the intrinsic worth of precious metals or gems. Honestly, the real value is preserving the site *in situ*, which undoubtedly is the reason the Venezuelan Army had been put here to begin with.

Noble cause, but geez. Talk about a crappy assignment. This is totally a 'middle of nowhere' post. Even the old airfield in Alaska was only twenty minutes away from a pizza place, not a ten hour walk through thick-ass jungle. Though, to be fair, I imagine the military air-drops supplies via helicopter.

My amplified hearing lets me avoid a handful of mortals patrolling the perimeter of the temple grounds. Three small squarish stone buildings roughly the size of my detached garage stand on the north, east, and south of a five-story ziggurat.

Though the buildings all have a thick coating of jungle growth, moss, and other green stuff, the land between them has been largely cleaned out—probably the military's doing. Rough-cut vines jutting out from the vegetation on the buildings makes me think this entire temple complex had been swallowed whole by the jungle for many years.

Not to be too superstitious here, but the place *does* give off a weird energy.

I'm probably picking up Elizabeth or Izeth… or whatever magic they're using. Humans haven't sincerely believed in Incan gods for a long damn time. Wonder if stuff stops existing if we give up on it? Like, in the highly unlikely event all of humanity decides to stop thinking of the Devil as a real being, would he go *poof*?

I didn't know, but if any Incan gods still existed, I'm sure they'd be plenty pissed off about Elizabeth and her crew apparently taking over one of their temples.

Meanwhile, two mortal soldiers appear around the corner of the nearest small building and end up staring right at me.

Oops.

Time seems to drag to a standstill as my reflexes kick up to the max. I rush at them before they can shoot, grabbing their rifles, yanking the weapons out of their grip, and launching them into the nearest stone building. The men draw in air to shout. I grab them each by the face with my hands, covering their mouths, and shove them hard into the vine-covered stone.

They both slide down the wall, out cold.

Squish. Muddy footstep behind me. I spin around.

An olive-skinned woman in her late twenties is standing there, looking like she walked off the set of a stage production of *Cleopatra*. As in, her revealing white outfit resembles a modern take on trying to look like a garment from ancient Egypt. Sadly, the faint shimmery light aura of an ascendant dark master surrounds her body.

She extends her claws. “You should not be here.”

Crap. So much for stealth.

Chapter Five
Subtle

I tilt my head. “Technically, you shouldn’t be here, either.”

The woman, about to lunge at me, pauses. “Of course we should.”

“Not really. You basically stole the place from the Venezuelan Army and whatever Incan gods live here. You’re about to invade another world. If you’re going to start tossing around lines like ‘you shouldn’t be here,’ at least be accurate about it.”

“I grow bored of your word games.” She thrusts her arm out, lime green energy surrounding her fingers.

Expecting her to throw something, I dive to the ground.

… and I’m covered in snakes.

A dozen or so black serpents bigger around than my arms sprout up from the ground like tentacles, some wrapping around me, some biting. I manage not to scream despite having fangs the size of ice-picks stuck in my body.

Kingsley jumps at her, still in wolf form. I'm vaguely aware of an orange energy bolt flying from her hands and the meaty slap of a heavy body hitting stone. Kingsley turns, snarling.

Burning pain spreads out from wherever the snakes bite me. Great... venom. I grab the neck of a critter chewing on my left shoulder and squeeze until its bones shatter. The instant its neck breaks fatally, the entire snake disintegrates into smoke. The remaining fourteen or so don't seem to notice or care.

Kingsley growls again. I can't see a damn thing with my face in the underbrush and a snake wrapped around my head, but it sounds like he leaps at the dark master and scores a hit. She grunts in pain. The scent of foul blood reaches my nose along with the gurgling noises of a nauseated werewolf.

Fortunately, I have experience fighting a grabby, multi-headed, aggressive conjured blob of enchanted serpents. Yes, I'm talking about PTA meetings. At least here, I don't have to hold back. Claws out, I grab, break, and shred at the snakes.

What the hell is it with dark masters and tentacles? Do they like them because they're creepy and weird? Okay, snakes instead of octopus suckers is worth style points at least, but I could do without the flesh-dissolving venom. It hurts so much it doesn't hurt, if that makes sense. My brain just closed the *nope* gate on that feeling.

Know what's highly disturbing?

Six small holes in my skin making gurgling noises because the venom clashing with my healing ability is releasing steam. One by one, I tear apart the snakes holding me down. I sit up, gasping, and see that the ascendant's once-white dress is thoroughly covered in blood. Well, at least her skirt is. No damn clue where the top went. Probably in Kingsley's stomach. Speaking of the big guy, he's upside down about twenty feet away, sliding to a stop against a tree.

The woman holds up her right arm, which stops existing a few inches in front of her elbow. She looks furious, and glares at the bloody stump—as it regenerates out to a new hand in only as long as it takes me to scramble back to my feet.

Holy shit… has Kingsley been biting giant chunks out of her the whole time?

She raises both hands at him, grumbling in not-English. Pale ghostly light gathers around her palms. No idea what she's doing, but I know I don't want it hitting Kingsley. I charge into her from behind, body-checking her. The pale energy beam swerves into the jungle, striking a tree—which promptly dies. In seconds, it goes from a live tree to something apparently dead for ninety years.

Eek!

"Elizabeth should have done this as soon as she escaped." The ascendant points at me. Her hand turns into a snake head.

I dive to the right as an anaconda-sized reptile launches like a missile. The huge serpent passes over me by mere inches as I swoop in and grab her by the throat, lifting her off her feet. The blood coating her bare chest glistens in the moonlight.

"If you want to take a quick break to go put something on, we—"

She grabs the arm I'm holding her with in both hands. Sensing she's about to snap my forearm like a stick, I hurl her at a nearby stone building. She flies headfirst into the wall, bounces off, and hits the ground. For an instant, I think she might be unconscious, but she pushes herself up to her knees, her head swinging floppily on a broken neck.

Mom! says Tammy in my head. *Elizabeth knows we're here.*

I sigh. So much for being subtle. Figures. As soon as this ascendant saw us, Elizabeth would have known.

You guys might as well join the party, I think.

We're already on the way. And eww! Her neck is all broken and stuff.

Kingsley runs in like a black furry missile, scooping the ascendant up in his mouth and damn near biting her in half at the waist. She hammer-fists him on top of the head, cracking his skull. The *snap* of bone is so loud I feel it echo in my spine. Kingsley crashes to the ground on his chin, out cold. The faux-Egyptian princess is stuck in his jaws, her body healing so fast it forces his mouth open wider. Already, her head's back on a solid neck.

She reaches down by her hip and grabs one of his giant fangs. The mere thought of her intending to break it hurts.

Dammit. No point being quiet now.

I charge in, drawing the Devil Killer out of seeming thin air. Unlike demons, this bitch can't simply sense its presence. A faint grunt comes from her mouth as she pulls at the fang, trying to snap it. I'm so focused on spearing the blade into her back, she catches me off guard by thrusting her foot out into my shin. I trip, instinctively throwing my arms forward to catch myself instead of stabbing her, and land draped over Kingsley's head, partially on her, likely driving his teeth into her a little deeper. Good.

She grabs my hair, yanking it hard enough to fling me into the air. I go spinning horizontally until I smack into a tree, then crash to the ground.

Burning creeps across the back of my skull. Has to be a torn scalp. I reorient myself, looking back at them just as she grabs Kingsley's fang again.

I raise my left hand to project a magical bolt. My baseball-sized yellow light glob smacks her upside the head with a crackling zap. Her hair fluffs up. She blinks, gives me this 'are you serious' sort of stare, then lets go of the fang to hurl an orb of fire as big as a basketball in my direction.

Fortunately, the incoming fireball does not have vampiric speed. It's not even as fast as a bullet. I roll aside, leaving the incoming spell to hit the dirt. By the time I'm on my feet, she's extracted herself from Kingsley's mouth, thankfully without breaking his teeth. He's still out cold. Despite knowing he's a werewolf and nothing short of silver in the heart or a flying leap into a magma pool can kill him, the sight of a dent in the top of his head is horrifying.

She sneers at me, raising both arms. Flames weave around her fingers, spreading down to her torso, gathering brightness and intensity. Uh oh. Nothing that takes time to build up is going to be pleasant. It is probably a super bad idea to stand still. Gotta catch her off guard. Still holding the sword, I sprout wings and leap straight up. She unloads a massive barrage of flamethrower at the ground under my flap-assisted leap. I lean forward, flying in an arc, stabbing downward at her chest.

The ascendant scrambles to the side so fast she blurs. My sword misses nicking her arm by inches. Hoping not to give her the chance to throw more magic at me, I spin into a slash, cringing at Sebastian's imagined voice scolding me for slicing with a longsword. Only, the Devil Killer isn't a true longsword. It's not exactly a broadsword either. Sorta in-between. Besides, this dark master bitch isn't wearing armor.

She is, however, astonishingly fast.

I swing and slash over and over. She legit *Matrix* leans out of the way every time. I feel like an elderly woman with poor eyesight trying to whack a frantic cat with a broom. At least I'm pressing hard enough she doesn't have a chance to stuff another enormous snake up my nose.

"You are going to d—" She gives a yelp and falls sideways.

As she does so, I lunge at her, running her through the heart without the least bit of hesitation. Her body is dense and squishy, as though I'm forcing a blade into overly thick ballistic gel. I don't think ordinary human strength would be capable of harming these ascendant masters using a blade.

Grunting, I grab the handle in both hands and shove downward.

She gasps, shrieking in pain as her skin ignites around the sword. For an instant, her expression becomes one of sheer terror. This arrogant wench stares up at me like a frightened teenage girl, then abruptly disintegrates into a black, ashy-fanged skeleton. My sword seems to draw the essence of the dark master out of the disintegrating bones in vaporous tendrils of bright white energy. They swirl around the blade, seeping into the edge, heating it to a dull orange glow.

Kingsley grumbles something incomprehensible and spits out ash. I glance over at him. Seems he bit her on the ankle as she went by, tripping her and giving me the opening I needed.

"Elizabeth knows we're here," I whisper.

"What is it the kids say these days?" asks Kingsley, after shifting back to human. "Ya think?"

"Not funny." I stand straighter, clamping a hand over the back of my head, waiting for my scalp to mend. "It worries me we aren't getting swarmed right now."

Kingsley grabs his forehead in both hands. "Wouldn't it worry you more if we *were* being swarmed?"

"Probably, but I wouldn't have the time to think about much. I'd be too busy trying not to get killed."

He chuckles, then gestures at the ashes. "Did we win or just get our asses kicked?"

"She's dust and we're not. So, yeah, we won, but there are plenty more where she came from."

"I can't wait." He rolls his shoulders. "Please tell me she was extremely old and they're not all that fast, strong, and full of magic."

"No idea. This is all new to me, too." I let my arm fall at my side once the back of my head stops hurting. Not really sure how long it will take for my hair to grow back, but at least my scalp is well on its way to healing.

At the snapping and crunching of numerous people approaching, Kingsley shifts back to wolf form, saying it's better than standing there naked.

I can only agree.

Chapter Six
Senseless

Max emerges from the jungle, leading his people, including my kids and Allison.

Anthony's already gone Fire Warrior. Tammy follows him close, no longer 'out of it' due to concentrating on hiding us. It scares the shit out of me to have her here, but leaving her alone in the jungle is a sucky option, too. Allison's hands are already glowing, ready for battle.

Before I can say a word, the intonation of a dozen chanting voices rises up on the other side of the ziggurat. Not good. What I'm about to do is probably the dumbest damn thing I'll ever try, but maybe I can still catch her off guard.

"I'm going after Elizabeth," I say, drawing my sword. Before anyone can complain or stop me, I summon my wings and jump into the air.

I cruise up and over the huge overgrown

pyramid-like building. The jungle behind it glows, awash in lavender light. Izeth hovers by a pair of new-looking stone pillars, the 'fabric' part of his body fluttering as if in a strong wind despite the air being calm.

Elizabeth stands beside him, eyes wide in anticipation.

Six mortal soldiers are tied to trees in a circle around the pillars. Somewhere around fifty or more ascendant dark masters gather near the almost-portal. No sooner do I crest over the top of the ziggurat and take in the scene, than six of them slit the throats of the humans.

And they weren't the first; others lie dead around the scene.

Sweet mama.

As I swoop in closer, lightning bolts fly from the chests of each dead man, hitting Izeth before continuing on into the pillars. A brilliant curtain of electrical arcs leaps back and forth between the stone structures, merging into a rectangular hole in reality, revealing a desert landscape in another place. Izeth collapses in on himself, growing smaller and smaller, apparently joining the lightning bolts feeding the spell. Either Elizabeth screwed him over big time, tricking him into expending his life force to open the portal, or he simply went through it first.

Dammit!

There are at least fifty ascendant dark masters down there. Plus Elizabeth herself.

Screw it. I can teleport.

I dive at her, trying to be fast and quiet.

Ascendant dark masters rush for the now-open portal.

The Light Warriors spill around the corner of the ziggurat. About a third of them fire crossbows into the crowd of ascendants. Wails of agony beneath me are so intense it can only mean silver-tipped bolts.

Bright orange with fire, Anthony charges in on them like a huge, flaming boulder. My son lights up the jungle night.

Elizabeth is momentarily distracted by my son's rather epic appearance and doesn't notice me coming down on her from above. An instant before the Devil Killer sinks into her chest, another ascendant leaps in front of her. My sword punches through his chest instead, still hitting Elizabeth, but in her stomach rather than her heart.

As he collapses, his weight on the blade drags it down, slicing the hole in Elizabeth's stomach deeper until the tip hits bone and bounces out of her body. The man who blocked me flops around on the ground like a fish out of water. My strike didn't quite hit his heart, so he's still alive, but I think he's discovering my sword is a bit more than the average steak knife.

Elizabeth gawks down at herself, regarding the slash from below her right breast down to her hip with about the same level of shock as if I'd crashed into her at Starbucks and dumped a latte all over her. "What are you doing, Samantha? Betraying me after everything?"

"I can't betray you. We were never on the same side."

Crossbow quarrels whiz in behind me, raising the hairs on the back of my neck. I'm still technically a vampire. Silver will no doubt mess me up all the same. Some Light Warriors plus Allison lob fireballs and energy bolts at the ascendant Masters… who seem mostly interested in getting through the portal as fast as possible rather than turning and fighting. Still, some retaliate with magical bolts, summon serpents, or conjure rock spires up from the ground like huge earthen daggers.

"This is not your concern, Samantha." Elizabeth raises a hand. "Leave us be."

An invisible force crashes into me, hurling me backward. Since my wings are out, I catch myself hovering rather than eat dirt.

"I am leaving this world," says Elizabeth. "Are you never satisfied, child?"

"I can't let you enslave an entire innocent civilization," I say. "And I'm not a child."

She shakes her head. "I thought you were the smart one in your bloodline, Samantha Moon. You are in no position to tell me what I can or can't do. And you are certainly in no position to stop me."

"My sword says otherwise."

Meanwhile, the Light Warriors lay down an impressively consistent barrage of silver-tipped bolts. Unfortunately, their accuracy sucks. As far as

I can see, not one hit has been fatal. Then again, these ascendant ones are *fast.* Shooting them with crossbows is about as difficult as trying to hit a sprinting dog with a paper airplane. The only reason anyone hit anything is firing into a huge crowd. As the ascendant dark masters thin out, fleeing into the portal, fewer and fewer bolts find targets. Some of the ascendants drag themselves along the ground, their legs deadened by an embedded quarrel.

I'm sure the Light Warriors firing the crossbows can't see much in the dark, even with my son lighting the place up Burning Man style.

Elizabeth raises her arm, throwing a legit lightning bolt at me.

I get a real good close-up look at it, too. My wings aren't the most agile things in the world. I'm much faster on my feet in terms of dodging side to side. To be fair, if I'm flying forward at high speed, I'm pretty nimble, but hovering? Not so much.

That said, the lightning bolt hits me square in the chest, knocking the wind out of me—a weird sensation since I'm not sure if I have to breathe. In an instant, I'm on the ground with no memory of falling fifty or so feet. My chest hurts in a burny sort of way, but mostly I'm knocked senseless. The last time I felt anything like this, my older brother Dusk swung a door open in my path when I ran through the house. I must've been seven or eight years old at the time. Not even sure what made me run. Mom didn't want us running in the house and my brother appointed himself enforcer. So, he lay in wait for me to zoom by and shoved the door open in my face. Heavy wooden door, too. Knocked me right on my back. One instant, I'm running, the next, on the floor in pain. Felt like I couldn't breathe or move forever. Thought I was gonna die.

Speaking of which, I still owe him one. So not cool.

Elizabeth apparently finds me crashing in a heap of feathery wings hilarious. "Like a bird flying into a window…"

Someone running by trips over me and slides. I can't tell which side they're on. Grr. I drag myself upright.

Anthony's decided to resume his youth soccer heyday and is playing goalie by the portal, grabbing and throwing any ascendant dark master trying to make a run for the portal away from it. It's nerve wracking to see a large group of them all staring at my son with murder in their eyes… and also bewildering to watch them behaving as if afraid of him. I mean, these beings are *powerful*.

I tuck my wings in to keep them safe, and focus on Elizabeth, feeding on her mental energy. Her eyes flutter from the draining effect. I burn as much power as I can to make myself temporarily stronger, faster, and tougher. This effectively makes me hungrier so I can siphon even more energy out of her.

She finally seems to realize what's happening and lets out a bellow of rage. In a green flash, her Damascus scimitar appears in her hand, probably a conjuration. She runs in with a feinting high strike.

It's transparently false, so bad she realizes I'm onto the ruse and doesn't even try the real swing after. We circle for a second or two before she swings again. It's not a difficult block; I turn the strike aside and go for a thrust at her chest. Expecting it, she throws herself sideways like a matador.

Having used up so much energy on speed and strength, I'm basically even with her, but I'm only going to stay this jacked for about two minutes. Given we're an even match physically, it comes down to actual skill—and there, I've got the advantage. Elizabeth used to be some kind of cult priestess. She had minions to do the real fighting for her. However, for a sorceress who sat in the back and told others what to do, she *can* still fight.

The fifteenth time our blades clang off each other, I'm certain it's her sheer drive to not fail so close to realizing her goal keeping us stalemated. She briefly gets a far-off look in her eye, which I attempt to capitalize on. Her parry is slow, but still effective enough to stop me from landing a killing shot. Despite the gash to her left shoulder looking horrendous, she shows no reaction of pain or even annoyance, merely this creepy smile.

Okay, I'm skeeved. I can't see a gaping sliced-open shoulder and a dark smile as though she enjoys the pain and *not* squirm. She presses an attack, forcing me to yield ground in order to avoid getting sliced up. Defending forces me to keep looking at her wound and cringing in sympathetic pain.

Just as the wound heals, a flash of silver passes

between our faces. Sweet shit, someone nearly shot me with a silver bolt. I don't have time to scream 'watch it' at the Light Warrior who tried for Elizabeth's head since she goes into this batshit crazy dervish.

Nope. Not even gonna try parrying her. I jump back rather than attempt to cross blades with someone moving so damn fast. She chases me, keeping pressure on so I don't have a chance to focus on drinking more energy and boosting my speed again.

Tammy's scream pierces the chaos, my brain honing in on the one sound I fear most of all.

I can't help but spare a quick glance toward her.

My daughter is surrounded by a pack of knife-wielding human soldiers who have infiltrated the Light Warriors' ranks from behind. Elizabeth's mind-controlled minions are about to tear my daughter apart.

A blinding flash of white light detonates from Elizabeth as soon as I look away from her. For a split second, the image of ten stark white energy ley lines, like the spokes of an old wagon wheel, converge on the spot where the portal stands.

I brace for impact, expecting another feeling like a city bus doing fifty miles an hour slamming into me… but instead, the ground falls out from under me and I find myself floating in an empty void. All the screaming and chaos of the fight melts into placid silence—

Until the roar of a violent explosion hammers my brain into tapioca.

Chapter Seven
Nightmare Farm

The next thing I know, I'm face-down in dirt.

Luckily, I'm still aware of existing, so that's good news. Whatever Elizabeth did, she didn't send me to the Origin, though my head is spinning so hard the mere thought of standing up makes me want to hurl.

So I lay still, listening to the wind in the trees for a moment. Sure, it's probably stupid of me not to move, but I'm clearly not where I was before. And if the dirt presently caressing my face *does* belong to the Venezuelan jungle at *Kancha Huanca*, everyone else there—good guys and bad guys—is either severely unconscious, dead, or blasted elsewhere.

It would *not* be this quiet if anyone still fought… or even moaned in pain.

The dizzying haze of whatever force slammed

into me finally lifts. I no longer feel like one of the kids at the party Tammy called me for help from. Standing is possible, but I'm still afraid to. It's too quiet. If I lift my face out of the dirt and see my kids' lifeless bodies, I don't trust myself not to end it all.

But I can't lay here forever though.

My gut twists into a knot, but I push myself up.

Dread evaporates the instant my brain processes these surroundings. I'm no longer in Venezuela's jungle, but a pine forest in a ditch by the side of a two-lane road. Explains the silence.

And… I'm alone. Okay, this is different.

I stand and look around. It's dark, but my eyes can see without a problem. Trees line the road on the right side, to the left stretches a vast swath of farmland lush with various vegetables in their full, leafy glory. Almost a mile away on the other side of the field, I see a familiar farmhouse and garage. It takes me a second to wrap my brain around *why* it looks so familiar.

You bitch.

Elizabeth teleported me back to Northern California. I'm right next to Elliston's farm. This is the place I used to steal from as a little kid. My childhood home is right up this road about half a mile or so.

Very freakin' funny.

I picture the battle site in my mind and call the dancing flame.

Or try to.

It doesn't appear.

Grr.

I concentrate harder… still nothing.

Talos? You there?

Silence.

I mentally shout *Talos?*

No reply.

"Okay, bitch. You hit me with a spell that turned off my powers."

I try to spread my dark angel wings. Okay, those work.

Hmm.

Claws?

Those work, too.

Like a kid about to shoplift, I glance around to make sure no one is watching, then try to pinch the guardrail beside the road. The steel bends when I give it a decent push. Okay, I'm still strong. So, she kicked me across the globe and somehow nerfed my ability to teleport. I mutter "bitch" about a dozen times to myself and pull out my… Dammit! I left the cell phone in the hotel room.

Yeah, I'm stranded in NoCal. Wings work at least… it'll take me a couple hours to fly home at 120 or so miles per hour, but it beats walking. I have a spare work phone there.

What's going to absolutely suck is having no idea what's happened to my children, Allison, or Kingsley until I can get to my phone, since I don't actually remember any of their numbers by heart. Yes, I fail.

Grumbling, I dip my knees, about to leap into the air, but catch sight of motion on the road. Someone's coming toward me. They haven't seen me yet, so I put the wings away and crouch. A small head of dark hair rises up from a dip in the road. A pale, barefoot little girl in a threadbare beige dress creeps toward me as if trying not to be noticed. She's about nine, looks dirty, thin, and possibly malnourished. Aww. The sight of her makes me want to scoop her up and buy her a decent meal. Or, since my purse is hundreds of miles away, mind-control someone into feeding her.

The child keeps pausing to look at the farm. Heh. Guess kids are still at it. Lots of poor families live around here in the woods. So damn far away from any sort of civilization the real estate's cheap. Well, cheap for California anyway.

When she gets to within about thirty feet of me, the child looks in my direction, but doesn't see me —no surprise considering it's dark. However, the instant I get a good look at her face, it feels like someone's dumped a bucket of ice water down my back.

I'm not looking at some random little waif.

It's *me.*

This scrawny little dust rat sneaking down the road is freakin' *me* at nine years old.

I gaze up at the darkening sky. Oh, dammit, Elizabeth. What the frick did you do?

The child gasps.

I look down from the stars.

She's spotted me and has frozen in place, trying too hard to act casual. I don't need powers of mind reading to know the guilty face. Between having raised two kids and the minor fact of this being *me,* I know exactly how she's thinking: wondering if I caught her trying to sneak onto the farm or not.

"Hi," whispers child-Sam.

Normally, I'd ask her why she was out wandering on the road at night. Did Elizabeth punt me into her portal with a bit of backspin? Have I landed in an alternate dimension or simply gone back in time? Wait, isn't meeting yourself in the past supposed to be like incredibly bad? Well, I suppose since we haven't annihilated each other already, it's safe to talk. Plus, hadn't I seen myself in Richmond, Virginia, back during the Civil War? I had. Now *that's* another story for another time.

No point asking her why she's out here. I already know. "Hey."

Child-Sam narrows her eyes at me, perhaps confused at the casual greeting rather than a grown-up giving her grief for being outside so late.

"Do you know what time it is?" I ask.

She sighs, giving me a 'here we go' expression.

"Seriously," I say. "I left my phone at home. Don't know what time it is."

Child-Sam tilts her head. "Umm… everyone leaves their phones at home, duh. They're part of the wall. Why would you take it with you? And what does a phone have to do with telling you what time it is? Do you call someone to ask or something?"

Ugh. I pinch the bridge of my nose. This is like 1984 or so. Cellular phones wouldn't exist here. "Never mind. Weird dream. It's gotta be after eleven if you're out here scoping Elliston's farm."

She gets paler. "Scoping?"

"Relax. I don't care. I used to swipe vegetables from this place as a kid, too."

Child-Sam gives me this bug eyed 'holy crap, really?' stare. "Mr. Elliston is a butthead! He has this huge farm and all these veggies but he doesn't share."

"I hear you, kid. And here's a secret I haven't told a lot of people, if any. I used to laugh at him when he fell down the stairs on his back porch. Every darn time his dogs started barking at me, he'd come running outside. They'd always tangle him up in their leashes and he'd go rolling down the steps."

She starts to giggle, but clamps a hand over her mouth.

I'd been knocked back in time before, thanks to the mother of all voodoo curses. I'd also gone forward in time thanks to both ley lines and a time travel ring.

Had I been knocked back in time... or knocked into a parallel world?

Or both.

I glance at the farm. It's been so long, but the place looks exactly like I remember it. No wait... it's bigger than I remember. And wasn't it pale white all over? This has black trim around the window. Hmm, now I wonder if Elizabeth somehow knocked me so dang loopy that I ended up in an, I dunno, alternate reality or something not quite identical to my version of Earth. If I really am in an alternate universe, what else could be different here? Like, maybe the South won the Civil War. Or America never broke away from England. Or maybe the guy who assassinated Archduke Ferdinand missed and World War I never happened… which prevented World War II from happening.

Maybe this world has cold fusion tech.

Doubtful, since there are no cell phones yet.

But not everything is different. In fact, I'm pretty sure I remember the dress child-Sam is wearing. It used to be Mary Lou's.

"Hey…" I look at the kid. "Is the zipper on your dress broken? Does Mary Lou safety-pin it shut for you?"

She gasps again. "How do you know that?"

I shrug and smile. "I'm good at guessing stuff."

Something large and black moves behind the rows of cornstalks. I peer toward it and barely hold in a scream at the sight of an enormous fanged rabbit bigger than most passenger cars. Its four glowing red eyes glare malevolently at me as if daring me to venture into the corn so it can eat me. The initial shock at seeing the giant evil rabbit wears off in a few seconds. After going down the throat of a demonic dragon, a sedan-sized bunny shouldn't even make me raise an eyebrow. Only reason it did is… this thing's from my childhood nightmares.

After the first time I swiped veggies, I started having nightmares of various monsters lurking in the vegetable patches. Looking back on it now, they probably came from my immature mind conjuring them up out of some vague sense of dread at being caught stealing.

Child-Sam can't see the bunny. She's still a mortal without night vision abilities.

But in this world... the damn thing is real. What the hell is going on? Were my nightmares as a kid somehow inspired by real monster rabbits living in a similar, alternate reality? Real in one world, but nightmares in the other? Or maybe I'm simply hallucinating them now. I stare at the monster, daring it to do something… and notice it isn't making any of the plants it touches move. Either it's a spirit rabbit from hell, or all in my mind. At that thought, I become vaguely aware of a mild pressure on my head… not physical pressure, it's similar to the way it feels when a vampire tries to use compulsion on me not realizing I'm a vampire, too. The instant I realize an external force is attempting to affect me, the shadow-bunnies disappear.

Grr. What the hell? Who is trying to freak me out? Child-me isn't throwing off any unusual energies. Can't be her. She also didn't react at all to me breaking past the 'fear' effect. Is there a dark witch around here using terror magic on me? How could they know I'm here?

Right… I'm totally *not* in Kansas anymore in every way possible.

"Hey, you kinda look like my mom. Are you her cousin?"

"No…" I climb up out of the roadside ditch, approach my younger self, and crouch down to eye level with her. "Hi, Sam. I'm Sam, too, and this is gonna sound strange..."

Chapter Eight
Grief

Blinding white light and weightlessness last a few minutes before gravity returns.

Anthony falls flat on his chest, landing on a smooth floor with a *smack* like a big steak being slapped down atop a marble countertop.

"Ugh."

Distant voices float in and out of clarity over the sound of multiple television sets on different channels. A woman says something about Room 213 while a man on the phone asks about a dosage. Anthony doesn't need to look to realize he is naked. Cold floor touching him everywhere already tells him he'd snapped back from the Fire Warrior form reflexively… or as a result of whatever the hell had slammed into him. An explosion, maybe.

Where the heck am I?

Hospital, I think, says Dad. *You're in the middle*

of the hallway. Get up and find some clothes before you get caught.

Grunting, Anthony pushes himself up to one knee and looks around. He appears to be near the end of a hallway by an elevator. A few plain doors look like storage closets. Thirty feet away, two open doors lead to patient rooms. Problem... he can't really go far without being seen. Voices float from the distant end of the hall, some hundred feet away, where a nurses' station occupies an opening at a corridor intersection.

Shoot. He really, really doesn't want to be seen like this.

Randomly, Anthony dashes for one of the closet doors on the left. Locked didn't matter much… he pulls on the door until it breaks open, then slips inside, by some miracle having avoided anyone seeing him.

Alas, the room contains shelves of boxes, mostly cleaning supplies.

Next room to the right, says Dad. *Looks like a laundry room. Full of scrubs.*

"Bingo." Anthony approaches the door. "Let me know when it's clear."

The strange sensation of his father's vaporous essence projecting itself out of him accompanies a faintly visible shadow form wisping into being. He likens the feeling to pulling out one of those rubber-band boogers that felt as though it wrapped around his brain. Less pleasant was the goose-bump-raising chill and generalized ick. He loved his dad without question, but over the past year, whenever he did something like this—leaning out of the body or visibly manifesting—it made the hairs on Anthony's neck stand on end. Anxiety similar to getting caught stealing made him clench his fists. He hated that such apprehension came from his father's presence.

Go, said Dad. *Now. Hurry.*

Anthony pulls the door open and streaks the ten feet to the next closet, which hadn't been locked. He slips inside, shuts the door, and fumbles around for a switch. Once the lights come on, he breathes a sigh of relief at seeing shelves of folded teal scrubs. Stealing is wrong, but he can't exactly run around with nothing on. Helping himself to a pair of scrubs doesn't feel like too much of a bad thing. They're not exactly, ya know, valuable. Just crappy hospital clothing.

He hastily pulls on a set close to his size—not too difficult since he's had a growth spurt, and is as tall or taller than most grown men. In fact, his father's old clothes had even gotten a bit tight on him. And no, he wouldn't let his mother throw them out, which she wanted to do. Maybe someday, but not yet. Anyway, no shoes in here, but people wouldn't call the police on a guy walking around barefoot, would they?

Anthony still hasn't come up with a good excuse for the inevitable moment when a Fire Warrior session gets him stranded somewhere in the buck and someone catches him. How the heck would he ever explain that to someone and not end up sounding like a crazy person, a creep, or a druggie? The least bad thing he'd yet thought of would be to claim he got drunk at a party and woke up mysteriously naked. Hopefully, he'd never have to use it.

"Any idea where we are?"

Clearly, a hospital.

Anthony sighs. "You know what I mean. What city?"

Dad chuckles at the back of his mind. Dad didn't laugh much anymore. Watching his mother and Tammy going on as if he hadn't died—or they didn't care—had driven him into a bit of a depression. Anthony accepting him in spite of their present circumstances helped. His father initially tried to blame everyone but himself for his present semi-dead situation, but Anthony had set him straight about a year ago, refusing to back down. After all, Danny Moon had done this to himself. Anyway, his father finally accepted, or at least *said* he accepted responsibility, even admitted the rift with his mom had been entirely his fault.

It made sense, after all. Anthony couldn't really blame his father for freaking out at Mom becoming a vampire. What rational person *wouldn't* come unglued when simultaneously confronting the existence of the supernatural and believing they'd lost their wife? Up until recently, his father had been absolutely convinced Samantha Moon died and had been replaced by a monster who'd kill all of them the first chance it got. Not until he'd delved so far into the blood magic he'd stained his soul did he finally realize how vampires worked.

Yes, a monster had been in their house, but it hadn't *replaced* Mom. It hid inside her the same way Dad lurked inside him now. The most uncomfortable thing Anthony had ever endured was listening to his father cry when he described the night he 'accepted' Mom had died. She hadn't, but he'd convinced himself the woman he married lost her life while jogging and they'd brought 'something else' home.

For the past few years, Dad tried to act normal… well, as normal as one could from inside their son's mind. He no longer seemed to have such animosity toward Mom, more a flinch reaction. He knew he screwed up and feared trying to talk to her about it. No point in it really. So what if Mom forgave him? Not like Dad could move back in if they made up.

Dad was, in nearly every sense of the word, dead.

Tammy, being telepathic and not shy about using it had already been around and around in a few shouting matches with him. Anthony hated having two people in his head screaming at each other; plugging his ears did nothing to help. His sister was *still* pissed at Dad for making Mom so sad by keeping them apart, and worse—lying to them when he said Mom didn't want to see them or talk to them.

Maybe someday, Tammy would be open to his apology.

However, neither the unrest between him and Tam nor the silent friction between Dad and Mom explained his father's recent mood. No secret Mom had been a bit emo lately over Tammy's eighteenth birthday. Anthony loved his mother every bit as much as he loved Dad, but she needed to deal with them growing up. They wouldn't be little kids forever. Heck, neither he nor Tam were little kids *now*. Not that Mom did anything to be annoying, but seeing her sad bothered Anthony.

And he couldn't do anything about the sadness other than figure out a way to turn himself back into a little kid—both impossible, and also nothing he wanted to do. His only option was to try his best to cheer her up and tolerate the public hugs whenever she lost control.

Strangely, Dad hadn't said much about Jacky's death. The loss hit Anthony hard for the first couple days, but he'd coped… far more quickly than he expected or felt natural. Being responsible for the gym felt a bit like Mom's burden containing Elizabeth. He didn't *not* want to deal with the gym, more worried about screwing it up. Probably too big a responsibility for him now. After all, if he messed up and the gym failed, it would be like desecrating Jacky's memory.

Ugh.

Thankfully, Kingsley found a boxer named Emmett Floyd to help out. Now, Anthony didn't have to worry about the gym right away. He had time to still be a kid for at least two more years until turning eighteen… and he could gradually figure out how to run the place. Unlike Tammy, he didn't really want to go to college. His future already felt separated from the normal, mundane way of the world. Years to come would be filled with demons and other weird situations no degree would be the least bit helpful for.

Well, unless he went to Light Warrior school. Which he may or may not do. After all, why did he need Light Warrior school, when he was already fighting real world ascended dark masters, demons, zombies, and even the Devil himself?

Mostly, he didn't want to go to regular college out of laziness. No point busting his butt studying subjects he'd never use.

No, something pulled him in another direction. He didn't want to verbalize it a 'calling' or some cheesy thing like out of a movie or video game. However, with each passing month, the sense he had a particular path to walk on grew undeniable.

"Okay, pops. Can't stand in here forever. They're speaking English, so we're not in Venezuela anymore. Need to figure out where the heck we are."

Anthony shuts off the closet light and heads out into the hall. As long as no one looks down at his bare feet, he can pass for a low-level hospital worker. Luckily, the scrub pants are long, and only his toes jut out. Total strangers never guessed him only fifteen. And if he went a couple days without shaving, he could pass for twenty. In fact, he could almost grow a real goatee and mustache. Still patchy along his cheeks, though. Hopefully, that will grow in someday.

His father chuckles in his head, and assures him it will.

Since the elevator at the end of the hall only went up, he figures he is on the ground floor already, so he heads down the hall toward the nurses' station… at least until his father's voice comes from the first room on the right. Wait, what?

"… all they can do. It doesn't make any damn sense! How can they not figure out what he has?"

What the crap? Anthony blinked. *That dude sounds just like Dad.*

"I can't lose him. I just can't," sobs Mom.

Or at least, a woman who sounds an awful lot like his mother.

Anthony pads over to the door and peers in.

His parents—both of them—stand beside a bed containing a small boy, no older than six or seven. The child doesn't *look* terribly sick except for a mild paleness similar to a flu. His father seems younger than he remembers. Mom, however, looks weird. Kids at school had sometimes teased him for having a 'hot Mom.' A few even taunted him by saying his mom wasn't his real mother, but some young woman his dad rebounded with after his real mom left. Or some crap like that. For the most part, he ignored them since he had no reason to be upset or worried. Mom being a vampire explained her young appearance.

But… somehow… Mom changed.

This woman in front of him looks older than she should be. Mid-thirties at least—maybe even forty —with a few premature grey threads in her otherwise dark hair.

Oh, wow, whispers Dad in the back of his mind. *This is incredible.*

What's going on, Dad?

Do you remember how you got sick when you were little? Terminal, going to die?

Anthony swallows. He remembers enough. The disease hit him fast and sent him to the hospital. He remembers being there for days and feeling terrible. But it's all just a blur now. *Kinda. I know it's why I'm this weird sort of superhero thing.*

Dad let out a tearful sigh in his head, watching his physical-world copy comfort his mother. *This is the evening you would have died. I remember everything about it. The curtains, that coffee cup I left on the radiator. But something's wrong.*

Anthony creeps into the room, silent as he passes the empty second bed. *What's wrong?*

Your mother doesn't look right. She's older here.

Dad... is she somehow not a vampire?

I think you're right. We look about the same age.

Meanwhile, in the hospital room, Mom squeezes child-Anthony's little hand and also breaks down in uncontrollable weeping.

The sight of his mother so distraught stabs him square in the heart. He's never seen Mom cry so hard before. The kid in the bed looks *so* dang small. But he had been, what, seven at the time? Geez, I was a runt!

Your mother did something to save you... I never knew how to feel about it. Furious, thankful, resentful, overjoyed.

Anthony gulps. *Yeah, she used an amulet. A magical amulet.*

Partly. She'd come into possession of a ruby amulet capable of curing vampirism. She could have used it on herself to become mortal again. If she had, we'd never have had this crazy ass life... I never did understand why she didn't use it.

Anthony knows why, thanks to his sister helping him fill in the blanks later when he was older.

The ruby amulet had only been given to her the year before, by a UPS driver who had turned out to be a vampire hunter. His mom didn't know what to make of the amulet, and certainly didn't know how to use it. Only when he had become sick and she had gotten desperate, had she sought out the Alchemist at the library at Cal State Fullerton. Only then did she realize the power of the amulet. And she had chosen to use it on him, not herself. Strange to think that he had been a legit vampire for such a short time. Now, of course, he was something else.

Tammy filled him in on a lot of this stuff, and only recently, having waited for him to grow up enough so he could process it. Anthony knows his mother later came into possession of a fourth medallion. The diamond medallion. This is the one she returned to the Alchemist, having decided to not use it on herself. He knew his mom felt she had to stop Elizabeth. Mom thought she'd been chosen to bear a great burden. If she used the diamond medallion to cure herself, she'd have been releasing Elizabeth on the world.

Anthony looks down. Years ago, he sometimes wondered if Mom liked Tammy more than him. He'd come to brush the doubt aside with the rationalization Tammy needed more support. Anthony had always been strong inside. Watching his mother here falling apart so severely as she helplessly watches him die proves beyond any doubt she doesn't love him any less than his sister. Something tells him *this* version of his mother would never recover if she loses him now.

Dad's presence writhes inside him. *I can't...*

You can't what?

I can't sit here and watch this.

Except Anthony can't bring himself to turn away, hard as it is to watch. *Did we go back in time? Why isn't Mom a vampire? Is this some kind of dream, or alternate reality?*

Bingo. I think Elizabeth threw us sideways and we probably landed in a parallel version of Earth. Somehow, here, your mother didn't get turned into a vampire... and she never met Max. She doesn't have the ruby amulet. She can't stop you from dying.

Anthony fidgets. *Is this even real?*

I think so, kiddo. I can feel it's real. Different from our home dimension, but still real. And no, we aren't dreaming. You know I'm not in your mind when you sleep. I go back to the Void—or at least I used to before it broke. Now, I wander around the normal world.

Anthony nods. He knows this.

This is as real for them as our world is for us. I'm sure Elizabeth threw us into the interstitial space between dimensions, and somehow, we landed here.

Uhh, say what? Inter-stitch?

His dad gives off a sense of smiling. *Picture a drawer full of file folders. The folders are dimensions. All the air between the folders is the interstitial space. There are tens of millions of alternate realities all playing out in various ways. Some people think every significant choice we make spawns a new one.*

I dunno, Dad. Sounds kinda sketchy to me. One human being making an A or B choice isn't going to create a new alternate reality every time. Like if I decide to have pizza instead of a burger some night, it's not going to spawn a whole new world.

Heh. I suppose not. Maybe it's only significant moments more than a choice made by an individual... unless said individual is about to do something that will affect the entire world like assassinate Adolf Hitler, but chickens out.

Anthony scratches at his chest, forcing himself not to cry from watching his mother so destroyed at her helplessness to do anything to save her son. *Maybe there are legit alternate realities, but I don't think the permanent ones exist because people made smaller, insignificant choices.* Anthony pauses. An idea occurs to him that feels right. *Or, Pops... what if it's more like God playing video games and going through them over and over again... but making different choices to see what happens?*

His dad gives him a mental shrug. *Could be. Son, I want to save you.*

I don't need saving.

Not you. The little boy in the bed. Seven-year-old you. Get closer. I can jump when he's inches from death.

What? No. Anthony clutches at his heart. *I can't lose you again. And not after Jacky.*

A tingling sensation manifests on Anthony's shoulder, as if his dad is squeezing it. *Ant... I couldn't have asked for a better son. You're a man, now. And no man needs their dad hovering over their shoulder constantly.*

Alternate world or not, the reality of what his father is saying begins to totally freak Anthony out. His father is leaving him? Like, legit leaving him?

Please, I'm sorry... don't leave. Tears gather and spill out of Anthony's eyes.

You don't have to apologize. You didn't do anything that made me want to leave. I'm not leav-

ing you, I'm saving a helpless version of you. He's still my son even if we're in an alternate reality. This Anthony needs me. I'm… I don't belong in your mind. I've imposed myself on you for selfish reasons. It's not fair to you.

Anthony shakes his head. *No, Dad. No. I don't mind. You're not imposing.*

Ant, come on. What kid weeks from his sixteenth birthday likes having his old man aware of his every move? You're not a child anymore. I'm messing with your life. It wasn't fair how I messed with it already. I never should've gone off the deep end, diving into this black magic bullshit trying to 'save' your mother when she didn't need saving at all. I can't drag you down with me anymore, kid.

"Dad…" whispers Anthony.

The younger version of his father turns, finally noticing Anthony in the room. It takes this version of his father a moment to recover enough composure to speak. "Are you in the wrong room?"

His alternate-mom looks up, dabbing tears. "Hello. What's your name?"

Anthony doesn't answer. Not yet. Truth is, he's not sure how to answer.

Ant, says his father in his head, *you will find a way back to our reality. Keep Tammy safe. She needs you.*

But she doesn't even like you.

Dad chuckles. *That's normal for teenage girls. Yeah… I know I screwed up. If I could do it all over again, I would have believed your mother when she told me, "I'm still me." God... it rips my heart out thinking about her then. I am such an asshole for doing that to her. I'd convinced myself I'd already lost her and I'd been too heartbroken to think straight. You have your own path ahead of you and... it's somewhere I cannot go.*

"Are you okay?" asks young-Dad. "You look a bit sick."

"Dad," says Anthony, talking to the voice in his head. "Please, it's too soon. Not after Jacky. I can't..."

"What are you talking about?" asks young-Dad.

Son, this is not goodbye. It's an 'I'll see ya later.' Talk to Allison. She can let you speak to me whenever you need to. Please let me do this. I cannot bear to watch this version of you die.

"But this isn't really me..." Anthony steps closer to the bed despite not wanting to.

His child self appears to be asleep, skin pale.

"Did you just call me, Dad?" asks young-Dad.

"It's, um, complicated." Anthony looks over at him.

"This is your sister's doing." young-Dad points at Mom. "She's messing with us."

Mom breaks down crying again. "No. She's not as evil as you think."

"Wait. Whoa..." Anthony gawks. "Aunt Mary Lou is a vampire?"

His parents stare in shock at him.

"How the hell do you even know her name?" barks young-Dad.

"I'm Anthony, but from a different reality." He rests his hand on his mom's arm. Her warm arm. "This is going to sound nuts, and trust me, I'm just wrapping my head around it, too. But in my reality, Mom, *you* became the vampire."

This dimension's parents gawk at him.

Young-Dad narrows his eyes in suspicion.

Anthony continues, relieved that they seem at least open to the craziness spewing from his mouth. "Not long after Mom got shot on a drug raid HUD assisted with, she went jogging late at night at Hillcrest Park. Still not really sure why she went out so late. But the vampire got her in the park. Well, two did. One evil one, and then shortly after, her one-time father. Kind of a long story, actually."

Mom covers her mouth with one hand, her voice a scarcely tonal rasp above a whisper. "Mary Lou's car broke down years ago in the middle of nowhere on her way home from her job at the movie theater. She was only nineteen when she was attacked... and."

"And turned," finishes Anthony. "I know how it works, trust me. She never had kids?"

"No, why?"

"She had three in my world. Has three."

"Well, Danny is afraid of her. Mary Lou said she had to contain it—whatever *it* is—and went somewhere far away to protect us." Mom puts a hand on little-Anthony's chest. "I don't understand what's happening. Nothing I'm trying works. This is a natural illness, but the spells aren't working."

"Whoa, you're a witch here?" asks Anthony. "Umm, I mean, you're kind of a witch in my reality, too. Sorta. Well, lately."

"I'd give up all my magic to save him." Mom covers her face with her other hand, weeps softly behind it.

"Are we having some sort of grief hallucination?" asks young-Dad. "Like, how are we seeing an eighteen-year-old version of our son now?"

Anthony looks down. "Dad, I'm only fifteen. Be sixteen in a couple weeks. I'm not a hallucination, but it's a really long story why I'm here. Can't stay long. I need to find a way back to where I came from."

Little-Anthony emits a distressed whimper, the first sign of him feeling pain.

Mom grabs his hand and burst into sobs, begging him to wake up, come back, stay with her.

Why did I have to die so young?

Dad sighs in his head. *I have no answer. If you believe in that stuff about destiny, then perhaps you did everything you needed to do in this lifetime.*

"Makes no sense," whispers Anthony, then thinks, *How can a little kid accomplish life goals by seven? I can barely even remember anything I did before like eight. So if I did everything I had to do by seven, does that mean Mom messed up the universe, somehow, by keeping me alive?*

I'm not sure, says Dad. *Maybe what's happened is exactly what the universe needed or wanted. As a child, your soul's purpose might have been speci-*

fically to go through this sickness so Mom could do what she needed to do.

But she couldn't have saved me without being a vampire.

True.

Then why is it happening in this reality if Mom's not a vampire and can't stop it?

A scary sense of calm comes from his dad. *We're here now, aren't we? Mom can't save you...*

"But you can," whispers Anthony, resisting the urge to cry at the idea of losing his dad for the second time so soon after Jacky. The sight of his alternate-mother crying this hard breaks the last of his hesitation. He can't be selfish at the cost of his parents going through so much pain. "Mom?"

His other-mother seems lost behind her hand, tears spilling out between her fingers.

"Mom," says Anthony a little louder. "You're not gonna lose him… or, me."

I love you, Ant, says Dad.

"Love you too, Pops." Anthony reaches out and rests his hand on the child's arm.

Child-Anthony squirms, lapsing into wheezing, rapid breaths. The parents in the room begin to panic, sensing the end. Both began shouting for a doctor, yelling 'no,' and completely freaking out.

Anthony stands there, calm as a statue, watching his younger self convulse in his death throes.

A faint burst of black vapor flows out of teen Anthony's mouth and nose, rushing down to the bed and seeping into the child. The elder Anthony grips the edge of the mattress, momentarily paralyzed by an icky sensation as though his lungs had been filled with gelatinous slime that rapidly extrudes out of him. When the tail end of the dark vapor leaves, a sharp jolt rocks his entire body, too much for his legs to tolerate.

Anthony slumps to kneel on the floor, clinging to the side of the bed, breathless.

The sheer power of the shock hits him like a hammer. Whatever force bound his father's soul to him had broken. It doesn't seem possible; after all, everything Mom ever told him about dark masters made it sound like the only way to sever the bond would be for the host to die. *For me to die.* Another version of him in the room at the brink of death shouldn't count as him dying. Or did it?

Then again, I'm not a vampire. I'm something else. Dad didn't make me into whatever I am... I was already it. Guess he only hitched a ride.

A doctor and two nurses run in.

Little-Anthony lies there, calm.

The doctor begins trying to resuscitate him, believing the boy dead.

Young-Dad forcibly pulls Mom away from the bed so the medical team can reach the child. She fights him, nearly scratching him in the face. Anthony pushes himself upright and helps this version of his father hold onto Mom.

"He'll be fine," whispers Anthony.

"He's dead, he's dead..." Mom sobs.

"Come on!" shouts the doctor at the inert boy,

his CPR growing aggressive. "Come on, dammit!"

"Ouch. Stop that," says little-Anthony.

Everyone freezes.

The boy makes a face as if someone whispered into his ear, then grins. He stares at the doctors and nurses for a long moment in silence. The medical team abruptly leaves the room without a word, seemingly confused. Mom ceases crying and runs to the bedside.

"What just happened?" asks young-Dad.

Though a ten-ton weight hangs on his heart at being separated from his father, he forces himself to speak. "In my reality, Mom became the vampire. You didn't handle it so well. Thought she was a monster. You guys fought a lot. Dad tried to get into black magic to 'fix' Mom, only he lost control and got himself killed. You turned into a sorta weaker dark master and have been sitting inside my head for a couple years now."

"You're a vampire?" whispers Mom.

"No..." Anthony sits on the end of the bed and explains what his real mother did for him. "I'm not really sure what I am to be honest. I'm still growing up, maybe too fast, too big, too strong..." He chuckles. "So I'm definitely not undead."

"Because you're still growing," says young-Dad.

"Right. Do you guys understand how dark masters work? As in, how they relate to vampires and stuff?"

His alternate-mother nods. "My sister told me

about it. They possess the living, turning them immortal, and sometimes taking them over completely."

"Err, right. So, my dad from my world just jumped into this little guy here so that you wouldn't lose him."

Hearing it out loud sounds worse than the reality of it. Basically, his dad made the decision to possess little-Anthony... rendering the child into... wow.

A vampire.

Maybe they should have just let the boy die. Ugh. But it hadn't been Anthony's choice. This was all his dad's doing, wanting to save the child, not being able to watch young-Anthony die.

I tried to stop it.

Anthony took a breath. "Yes, he's a vampire... for now. I suggest you find a man named Archibald Maximus. He can be found at something called the Occult Reading Room at Cal State Fullerton." Anthony explains further, about the magical room. He'd been there, after all, when he had inadvertently let loose a demon from a book. Alternate world mom seems to understand. Apparently, she's quite a powerful witch and grasps the concept of alchemy.

"For now, you'll need to keep little man here out of the sunlight. He's going to be awake all night because he literally *can't* sleep when it's dark. Dad, do you have a client named Jaroslaw here?"

Young-Dad blinked. "Whoa. How do you know that?"

"Guess our realities are kinda close." Anthony explained how the butcher provided blood for his mother to drink.

Alternate-Mom scoops the boy up and squeezes him. "Oh, God… he's so cold."

"Yeah," says Anthony, looking down. "Can't help that. Sorry."

"It's okay." Mom rocks little Anthony. "I couldn't bear losing him. Thank you."

Anthony looks back and forth between his mom and this version of his father. His child-self appears happy, if a little pale. Hopefully, Max could help him in this world. If Max was even in the area. After all, Anthony suspected Max was keeping tabs on his mother... and might be wherever Mary Lou was. Either way, his mother in this world was a witch. Perhaps she could use scrying to find the man. Of course, they would need to find the ruby medallion—or the diamond. Anthony nods to himself, suddenly confident. One way or another, little Ant was going to grow up... and perhaps someday even become the Fire Warrior in this world.

Did we do the right thing, Dad?

No voice in his head answered.

Tears gather in his eyes at his father's absence, but watching these parents hugging their son, so thrilled not to have lost him, gives him the answer he needs. Yeah… he had to let go of his father.

Little Anthony in this world needed him.

Goodbye, Pops.

The moment acceptance takes hold, the room around him drowns in blinding white light.

Chapter Nine
Little Spiteful

After all the things I've experienced in my life thus far, it takes a lot for me to think of something as being 'weird.'

Getting thrown back in time isn't weird. Been there, done that, got the souvenir musket ball with my name on it. Now, being sent to Northern California also isn't weird, merely unlikely. Some people look back on their childhood with a nostalgic yearning to return to simpler times. Not me. I'm glad it's over. And I'm not saying it for pity or because I have unresolved issues of parental neglect. My issues of parental neglect are resolved. I've dealt with them. Seriously. I simply act like my parents no longer exist—which isn't much different from how things felt in my childhood. The past is the past. I survived those years and moved on.

Having a conversation with my nine-year-old

self, however, counts as weird. Child-Sam didn't believe me at first until I brought up the 'hidden palace.' My grandparents on Dad's side were pretty old. Dad came along late. By the time I happened, the grandparents were halfway into their seventies. Mom's were much younger. I think they had her before they turned twenty… but Mom's grands are as spacy as her. Yeah, they're still alive, well into their eighties. Dad's parents died before I finished high school.

Anyway, where I'm going with this… my paternal grandparents knew neither their son nor my mother were really cut out to be parents. Before they got sick and ended up in a care home, they'd sometimes stop by and try to help look after us. My father resented their intrusion, so he had a nasty habit of taking away any toys or whatever they tried to give us unless they asked him permission first. Grandma snuck me a doll without telling him, and I concealed it from my parents in the crawlspace under the house, inside an old cabinet or something… wooden box with doors. Not sure what it used to be before it ended up under the house.

To my kid self, it became a doll's palace. I hadn't even told Mary Lou about it.

Since I knew about the doll under the house, plus the answers to every question she asked me, Child-Sam finally accepted we're the same person, though she thinks I'm from the future. Maybe I am. But something doesn't *quite* seem right here. I can't put my finger on exactly what's bothering me about this place or feeling abnormal. Or why it doesn't exactly feel in the past—probably because a seven-foot-tall black rabbit with fangs and four eyes never existed in my time.

Though it did in my dreams.

So flippin' weird.

Indeed, the creature confuses the situation away from simple time travel. At no point in the past did actual monsters roam this farm. At least, not unless Elliston's massive dogs count as monsters. They liked me, though, one reason I got away with stealing produce. Dunno if the dogs were trained not to bite kids, or they picked up on my witchy nature side.

"C'mon. We need food," whispers child-Sam. "Well, I do. I'm starving!"

Okay, that breaks my heart a little. I stand there for a moment unsure what to do as the little girl version of me slips into the roadside ditch, then climbs up the other side. She uses 'the spot,' a place where a gap in the dirt under the fence creates a hole just big enough for kids to sneak in.

Child-Sam pulls herself through, pushes up to squat, and peers back at me. "C'mon!"

There's no way I'm fitting under the fence. Oh, screw it. I extend my wings and fly over the ten-foot-tall monstrosity, landing beside her. Child-Sam gazes up at me in awe. As a kid, I always wanted to be able to fly. She probably thinks I'm an imaginary friend at this point.

Grinning, kid-me scurries off into the veggies.

I look around for the giant rabbit, but it's disappeared. Still feels like *something* is lurking around out of sight, watching us. The more I search for the origin of the unease, the more it starts to feel different… almost like an unpleasant task hangs over me. I crouch and follow child-Sam in among the rows of tomato plants. She picks one and starts eating it right there. Damn. How hungry I must have been to turn into a human gopher eating crops right off the vine. If memory serves me correct, we're going to steal zucchini and potatoes… something starchy since I'd already had to learn about nutrition somewhat. Something hearty. Cucumbers, I knew back then, are all water. Same for lettuce. Spinach is amazing, if she can find some.

While watching her eat, I ponder the mild dread sitting on my shoulders. Last time I felt like this, I had a certification test coming up for HUD. Like, I knew some serious studying had to happen, but kept finding excuses not to do it despite my job depending on passing the exam.

"Why do I feel like there's something I need to do?" I ask aloud, turning and looking around.

Child-Sam hastily finishes chewing. "There is. Grab veggies. And get down or he'll see you."

Ahh, childhood. We're almost a mile away from the house at night, among tall plants. Unless Mr. Elliston has night-vision infra-red cameras on the field, there's no way he's going to find us. Back then, I wouldn't have thought that. Adults all had superpowers. Especially nasty, greedy farmers.

This kid Ritchie who lived a couple houses away from us got caught stealing from the farm. Elliston pressed charges. Ritchie didn't go to jail or anything, since a couple of potatoes didn't amount to serious money, but his parents couldn't pay the fine. They lost their house and had to go to Oregon or something and live with the grandparents. Ritchie had been my friend, and because of this guy, I never saw him again. If I'm nine here, my friend has been gone for almost a year.

Child-Sam finishes her tomato and hurries deeper into the field, closer to the farm house. I walk after her, not intending to hide, but something about being here all over again makes me get down. This place has no fun, nostalgic memory. It's all desperation and fear and hunger. I'm overstating it, but the emotion I'm having right now is kind of like a tame version of a Vietnam vet touring a site where they used to sneak around in the jungle shooting at the enemy.

Part of me, I think, wanted to get caught so the cops would save me from a bad situation at home. The main reason I didn't simply go and ask for help is the fear my siblings would be separated. Though, I wouldn't necessarily have minded River going to live somewhere else, it would've killed me not to be with Mary Lou, Clayton, and Dusk. If I got in trouble for stealing vegetables—because Mom and Dad didn't buy enough food—whatever happened to us kids wouldn't feel like my fault as much as if I'd called the cops on purpose.

It's honestly amazing I ended up as a government agent. Samantha Radiance Sundance… With a name like that, I should've been the crazy woman at the end of the street with a house full of crystals, eleven cats, and a constant stream of local teens showing up to buy weed.

Basically, my mother except for the cats.

Child-Sam scurries around the farm the way I used to, plucking various veggies and using the front of her dress as a bowl to carry them. Once or twice, I got ambitious and stole a lot of veggies. Pulled a Clayton… took my dress off, made a bag out of it and streaked home carrying a Santa-bundle to feed the whole family.

So many hippies live around here, no one had batted an eyelash at me.

At the end of the cornstalks, child-Sam pauses, crouching low and staring at the farmhouse. She gets a weird glint in her eyes, looks at me, then transfers her stash of veggies out of her dress to a pile on the ground.

"What are you doing?" I ask.

The child grins at me, stands, and bolts off toward the house.

Whoa. Okay. Back in the day, I'd been morbidly afraid of going anywhere near the house… what's going on?

At least I can mind-control the farmer if need be. I stand and hurry after the kid.

She runs past the carrot patch, crosses a dirt lot where a bunch of farm trucks and tractors sit idle, and zips around to the side of the main house. The two big dogs on the porch don't pay any attention to her, or me, both seeming asleep.

I don't call after her for obvious reasons as I jog around to the back of the house. It's eerily quiet here, and now I'm *sure* this isn't coming out of my memory or imagination. At no time in the past have I ever been this close to the Elliston house, much less behind it. The level of fear this place once commanded was about the same as if it contained a factory that processed children into SPAM. I didn't want to get caught, killed, and turned into lunch meat.

Of course, nothing of the sort would've happened to me. I'm only saying how strong my irrational childhood fear of the place had been. Seeing child-Sam willingly run *to* this house is beyond wrong.

I hurry past a bench, a small well, and a butter churn (decorative, they don't actually use it) to the back door, which is open. When I reach the threshold and peer into the large kitchen, the stink of natural gas slaps me in the face. Hissing comes from the stove. Child-Sam's standing at the table, fussing with a box of matches while staring malevolently at a pair of candles.

What the actual fuck…?

Okay, whoa. This is *not* me. I'd never have done anything like this. Not even close. I wouldn't have even written rude words on their walls in crayon. Is this little demon version of me seriously trying to blow the house up? I really did used to resent Mr.

Elliston and his huge farm, all his money… but no way would I have tried to kill him.

"Stop that!" I whisper-shout while running in to grab her right forearm, keeping the wooden match away from the striker on the box. "What the hell are you doing?"

"I don't have to steal a couple veggies if we can take *all* of them."

"No. This is wrong. What happened to you, Sam? You're not like this."

"I hate him. He made my friend Ritchie go away forever." She narrows her eyes in anger. "Ritchie lost his house, so I want the mean farmer to lose his, too."

"Yeah, I remember. But this is wrong." I pluck the match out of her hand, take the matchbox from her other hand, and turn to shut off the stove.

The instant I let go of her arm, the *pffsh* of a match striking to life happens behind me.

I whirl in horror. Where the hell did she get another match from?

With a face as innocent as a faerie tapping a wand to a pumpkin, child-Sam stretches up on tip-toe to light one of the candles. Before the match even reaches the wick, the gas in the air ignites. Child-Sam shrieks in agony. Covered in flames, she stares at me in confused horror for a split second before the *whud* of an explosion knocks the crap out of me.

***

I'm flat on my back in a ditch beside the road.

The lingering stink of natural gas and charred flesh hangs in my nostrils, but fades in the span of two breaths... as if it never was. Child-Sam clearly hadn't expected the gas to blow up before she could get out. And… we died.

But, we didn't.

I *should* be screaming in agony in the middle of a house reduced to toothpicks. Even an undead psychic vampire should be seriously be hurting after such an explosion.

But I'm not...

In fact, no pain at all.

My ears pick up the soft patter of small bare feet on asphalt.

I sit up. Child-Sam, alive, unburned, and exactly as she'd been before we met, sneaks down the road toward me, heading for the gap in the fence.

No way...

I'm in one of *those* situations. Elizabeth threw me into some kind of *Groundhog Day* alternate dimensional reality. Little psycho-Sam is going to arson-murder Mr. Elliston and his family in this world. Again. It took me a long time to accept that the way my parents treated us as kids counted as a form of abuse. I never thought it screwed me up *too* much. Guess this version of me cracked. Now I understand where the feeling of having to do something came from.

This is some manner of trap. Elizabeth didn't

simply throw me at random into another dimension. I'm going to be stuck here repeating this moment over and over again until I do something 'right.'

What a bitch.

Chapter Ten
Reset

Okay, round two.

Maybe my adult-self presence here at the farm altered things. Maybe thinking she had a powerful friend (me) gave child-Sam the confidence to try and blow up the farmhouse. I didn't know, but as soon as she vanishes in the dip in the road and can't see me, I dart across to the opposite side of the street from the farm and hide among the weeds by the guardrail.

Child-Sam, oblivious to my presence, approaches the fence like I used to do, wriggles under it, and enters the farm. I extend my wings and fly into the air, observing her from the sky. She stops to eat the same tomato, then gathers the same veggies she did last time. The process is faster since she's not dawdling to talk to me. At the cornstalks, she pauses on her knees, staring at the house. Aww, crap. She's still thinking about arson.

Sure enough, the kid dumps the veggies out of her dress and starts running toward the house. I can't see her eyes from this angle, but I'm sure they're glinting with malicious intent. Based on what she said about wanting Elliston to lose his house, too, as revenge for what happened to Ritchie's family, I'm sure she's not wanting to murder the family, only blow up the house… unaware that doing so will cause them to die.

But, she's going to blow herself up, too.

Can't let it happen. Yeah, I know it'll only reset this weird scenario and she won't really die, but that 'what happened?' look she gave me in the instant before the explosion... yeah, it kinda kicks me in the feels. Plus, I'm pretty sure I'm supposed to somehow make this right. Or maybe not. Maybe this is Elisabeth's ingenious way to keep me busy for an eternity.

Either way, I dive after her like an eagle chasing a field mouse.

And, much like an eagle on a mouse, scoop her up and drag her into the air.

Predictably, she screams.

Lights come on in the farmhouse, but it doesn't matter. We won't be anywhere near the place by the time Elliston is outside. Aerial kidnapping—even if it's myself—is a new and awkward experience. Once the girl realizes we're 200 feet in the air, she stops squirming to escape and ends up clinging to me.

"It's okay, Sam. I'm not here to harm you," I say.

She doesn't respond.

I fly a half-mile or so down the road, then land before setting child-Sam on her feet. However, I still hold her by the wrist so she doesn't run off. We need to talk.

She sucks in a breath to shriek at me, but stalls in awed silence at the sight of my wings. "Are you an angel?"

"I am. Well, part time. But that's not the point. I'm here to tell you not to burn the house down."

Child-Sam trembles, shrinking in a little. Her posture says she's trying not to wet herself from fear. "I wasn't…"

"Shh." I guide her to the side of the road, sit, and pull her down next to me. "You're not going to get in trouble. You didn't actually do anything but think about bad stuff."

She gulps. Her trembling lessens, but doesn't stop. "I wasn't gonna do anything."

"Don't lie to me, Sam. I know. I'm you, all grown up from the future. I've come back in time to warn you not to try burning this place down."

"Umm." Child-Sam stares down at her lap, fidgeting for a while in silence. I recognize the gradual progression from denial to 'crap, I'm caught' to 'how can I weasel out of trouble' in her expression. "How did you know?"

"Already told you. I'm you… from the future."

"Nuh uh."

I point to her right knee. “River threw a stick at you while you rode Nicole’s bike. The stick went in the spokes and jammed up the front wheel. You went flying over the handlebars. Hurt your knee pretty bad.”

She gasps.

“Also,” I continue, “Nicole didn’t know you had her bike.”

“I didn’t steal it. Was gonna give it back.”

Heh. I smile. “Yeah, I know. She went with her family to Texas for two weeks.”

“Wow,” whispers child-Sam. “You know everything.”

I tell her about the hidden doll again, as well as a few other secrets only myself or Mary Lou would know. “You have to listen to me, Sam. If you try to burn the house, the gas is going to ignite before you can get away. It’s going to burn you, too.”

Child-Sam narrows her eyes at me. “Wait. If you’re me from the future, then I’m going to be okay. If I’m gonna die, I won’t have a future.”

I brush a hand over her hair. “Not exactly. The place will blow up before you can get away.”

“I don’t believe you. If I’m gonna die, you wouldn’t exist.”

“You’re smart.” I smile.

She shrugs. “Sometimes.”

“So… be smart now. Trust me. You don’t have to hurt anyone. What would Mary Lou say if she knew what you almost did?”

“Nothing.” Child-Sam scowls. “She’s gone.”

My heart stumbles a beat. "What? Gone?" I twist the little version of me around to stare into her eyes. "What happened?"

"She disappeared. I think she ran away." Little Sam looks away, clearly heartbroken. "I thought she loved me, but she doesn't care either. Just like everyone else."

I can't even picture Mary Lou abandoning me like this. I hug myself—not metaphorically—trying to comfort her. Something bad must have happened to my sister in this reality and their parents lied about it. My sister had been such a pillar in my life. Come to think of it, without her, maybe I would have gone to a dark place.

Oh, wait. Maybe this is what I have to do… find Mary Lou?

"Let's go look for her," I say. "Forget the farm."

"I still wanna blow them up. They're mean. They have so much food and don't share."

"No, kiddo. It won't help anything. Hurting people never does."

She squirms, trying to get away. "I don't wanna hurt them. Just blow up their house for being mean."

"Sam." I grasp her by the shoulders, forcing her to look me in the eye. "It's after eleven at night. They're all sleeping in bed. What do you think will happen to them if their house blows up?"

She blinks, bites her lip, then averts her gaze down. "Oh."

Hell with this. I can't leave my little self with

my parents. Something tells me they're even worse in this world. "C'mon, kiddo." I stand, picking her up.

"Where are we going?"

"Somewhere safe." I stretch my wings and leap into the air.

She doesn't tremble, but also doesn't look down.

It's been years, but I still remember the area. Orick, California is about ten miles southwest of here. Dad's parents live there. Once or twice, I daydreamed about running away and going to live with them. Wouldn't have really worked too well since they both ended up in a care home by the time I was thirteen, unable to live without assistance. Maybe it's different in this reality. Even if it isn't, having four stable years will make a huge difference in my—her—life. I'll drop her off, mind-control the grands to keep her, then go collect my brothers.

Maybe I'll mind-control River not to be such a dick while I'm at it.

Minutes later, I swoop in to land in my grandparents' front yard. The sound of a girl crying inside surprises me.

"Mary Lou!" blurts child-Sam.

Oh, wow. She's right.

I run up to the house, peering in the big window at the living room. A fifteen-year-old version of Mary Lou hugs both grandparents, tearfully pleading with them to 'get us out of there.' Her disheveled, dirty, and ripped dress makes her look as if she's been living on the street, but it's more likely she simply *walked* here and spent a night or two sleeping outside on the way. Damn miracle she made it here without getting abducted.

Child-Sam scrambles to get away from me, desperate to run inside and reunite with Mary Lou, almost like a little kid separated from their mother. I set her down on her feet and rush after her to the door.

She barges in. Both grandparents and Mary Lou spin toward her, shocked.

As I step across the threshold, my surroundings shift. The joyful sobs of child-Sam and Mary Lou, and the voices of my grandparents fade under the din of a tacky late-Eighties diner. I peer behind me at a set of aluminum-and-glass doors facing a downtown street. Klamath… the closest civilization to where I grew up. It's no longer dark, more like early evening.

Okay, weird. Well, at least I'm not in a ditch again.

Guess I passed the test, or whatever that was.

Hmm. Does it make me a wimp that I'm relieved not to have to fight the giant fanged rabbit?

Chapter Eleven
The Monarch

I stand a step or two inside the doors of a hauntingly familiar restaurant.

Can't really call it a restaurant *or* a diner. It's somewhere in between the two with traces of a Coco's, only without the giant cooler case of pies. The nauseating teal-and-white tile floor belongs in a hospital more than a room where people are supposed to be eating.

About a third of the tables—booths on the right, small freestanding tables on the left—are occupied. Everyone's got big hair and there's tons of denim. This has to be around 1988 or '89. Oh, crap. I remember this place… The Monarch. Klamath Glen is so small the only reason anyone even came here to eat is they only had one other choice, Crivelli's Bar. Not even McDonald's bothered with this place. Seriously, this 'town' isn't so much a town as a bunch of houses close together. Well, technically, The Monarch is in Klamath, which is about a mile up the road from Klamath Glen, basically its 'downtown.'

I'm guessing Elizabeth actually threw me into some kind of mental gauntlet. It would have been weird enough to land in an alternate dimension so close to my reality at all, much less it happening twice and both times at significant moments in my past.

A mental trial makes more sense.

I guess we'll see.

And, yeah, I remember The Monarch. I worked here during my last two years of high school.

Know what sucks more than being a high school kid waiting on tables? Having to ride a rusted bicycle five miles each way. I wasn't one of those kids whose parents made them get a job as a teen to 'learn how the world works.' We needed the damn money.

No one pays me any mind standing inside the door. Not surprising. People in this town seat themselves. I look around, trying to figure out what my 'task' is here, but no one really stands out. After a few minutes, another version of me emerges from the kitchen, carrying a tray with plates on it. Okay, based on the hair style, I'm ninety percent confident this is late in my senior year of high school. I'd be eighteen now, which means I'm in 1992. No surprise, The Monarch always did look a bit dated. They still had one of those physical credit card things we had to ram back and forth by hand to take an impression.

And, I see that I'm pissed.

Eighteen-year-old Sam is rocking a facial expression like the girl in the *Twilight* movie. She stomps across the room, putting on a false smile and politeness rather than slamming the people's food down in front of them. As soon as she turns her back on them, she starts crying. Careful not to look back at the seating area, 18-Sam hurries behind the front counter, grabs a plastic cup, and starts filling a soda for someone.

Oh, okay. I actually remember this day.

It's when I got into a giant argument with my parents about school. Neither one of them are what you'd call 'academically gifted.' Dad didn't even finish high school. He tended to think of anyone with an IQ in triple digits as bad or sneaky. Didn't trust them. Anyone who enjoyed reading books, he regarded as a 'free thinking intellectual who wants to destroy the country.' How messed up is it that my father got more upset at me *wanting* to go to college than he did at my brother Dusk ending up as a homeless, wandering artist rattling around Europe?

Mom didn't have anything against smart people other than not being one. She didn't see 'the need for' higher education. According to her, humanity did 'just fine' before they invented universities. Of course, humanity also used to burn people to death for suggesting the Earth orbited the Sun. So, yeah. This appears to be the day I told the parents my plans to apply for college and a few scholarship/ assistance offers, and… it didn't go well.

After like an hour of my father telling me I was too dumb for college and should be happy to be who I was and stop pretending to be something I wasn't, I stormed out and went to work in tears. Spent the whole night arguing with myself if my parents were right and I *was* too stupid for college.

Something tells me 18-Sam is going to do something reckless.

Dammit, Elizabeth. You couldn't have simply blown me up with a fireball. Had to stick me in some kind of weird 'this is your life and how it might have sucked if things went slightly differently' melodrama. Damn, wait. I hope Elizabeth did this and I *haven't* been blown to bits. Could this be what it's like returning to the Origin?

Crap. What if she *did* destroy me? What if this is the afterlife… well, what little of it I get before eternal oblivion? I'd expected nothingness or at least a momentary sense of total peace before the nothingness. So far, it's been anything but peaceful. Is it possible I might get a second chance or be allowed to reincarnate if I 'pass' these tests?

Hmm...

I hurry over to the counter by 18-Sam. "Hey, got a sec?"

She hides her face, pretends to be coughing.

"It's fine. I know you're upset because Dad's an asshole."

18-Sam stares at me. It doesn't take her long at

all to recognize me. Vampirism dragged me back out of my thirties and into my twenties... as far as looks go. Other than 18-Sam being noticeably slimmer than me—damn, love that teenage metabolism—we don't look too much different. I'm obviously an adult, not a teen, but we look so much alike there's no question in her eyes who she's staring at. Well, there is a giant question, but it's more of a 'how' than a 'who.'

"What the heck?" whispers 18-Sam.

"Kinda freaky for me, too."

Mack, the owner, emerges from the kitchen. He walks down the row of stools at the diner counter. I expect him to swerve around me but he doesn't—passing through me like I'm a ghost. Oh, this is beyond strange.

"Gnarly." 18-Sam leans back, wide-eyed.

Mack looks at her. "What? I got something on my shirt?"

"No. Sorry, I just… forget it."

"You okay?" he asks. "Your eyes are kinda red."

"Yeah, it's nothing. Just a fight with my parents."

Mack chuckles. "Gonna happen. Don't make the same mistake I did. Right now, they seem like morons, but when you're my age, you'll understand they were right." He points a finger gun at her, makes a clicking noise, and walks out the front door to meet the driver of a delivery truck loaded with eggs.

18-Sam sighs, staring down at the counter.

"In most situations, I'd say he's right." I shake my head. "But... our parents are not most situations."

"*Our* parents?" She scrunches her face at me, making the same expression Tammy does whenever she says 'what the hell are you talking about?'

Wow, Tammy is *so* my kid. Almost my twin.

"Hi, Sam. I'm Sam."

"Weird. We have the same name."

"Come on. You're a smart girl." I lean on the counter. "Look at me. Look at yourself in the mirror behind you."

She twists. Side by side, I look like an age progression photo of a missing high school senior. "Whoa, far out."

"Are you kidding? This is more than far out."

She blinks at me. "Are you seriously trying to tell me we're the same person?"

"I was about to, except I don't remember talking like a hippie from the sixties. When did you start saying, 'whoa, far out?'

"Umm, just now."

I cringe. Okay, *this* is how my present surroundings differ from actual reality. This girl is leaning more hippie stoner than I did for real. Or at least I did in my own world, assuming this isn't my end-of-life recap while the Origin reabsorbs me. The red around her eyes isn't entirely from crying, I notice. 18-Sam is half-baked.

Admittedly, I tried weed back then, but not

regularly enough to show up for work stoned.

"Okay, not a big deal. Just words," I say. "You could say I'm a future version of us. You just had a fight with our parents about college."

"Yeah." She takes the soda she filled and walks out from behind the counter.

I follow her to the table. "And you're going to spend all night working here debating with yourself if Dad is right or not."

"Here you go," says 18-Sam, plonking the soda down in front of a blond ten-year-old boy I don't know. "Need anything else?"

"No thanks." He smiles at her.

His mother nods at my teen self. "We're good for now. Thanks, hon."

"Groovy," mutters 18-Sam. She walks down the row, checking on people at various tables.

"Doesn't matter what Dad says," I continue, following her. "He's wrong. You *are* smart enough for college. We do get the scholarship, but it's not quite a full one. Still gotta work, but we make it."

"Greeeat," intones 18-Sam under her breath before asking two older ladies if they want more coffee. They do, so she hurries back to the counter to get the pot.

I wait for her by their table. On her way back, 18-Sam glares at me. The likeness to Tammy during her surly phase is uncanny. She refills the ladies' coffee, then goes two tables down to collect a pile of bills and a check from an empty table.

They left a $1 tip.

Oh, that had to be Mr. Marley. He always tipped like crap.

18-Sam sighs, stuffs the single note into her apron, and grumbles her way back to the counter.

"So…" I lean on the counter beside her as she runs the tab through the register. "I've been sent back from the future to make sure you decide to pursue college."

"Why bother?" mutters 18-Sam. "What if Dad's, like, correct? He said I'm not 'right' for college."

"He's full of crapola." I nudge her on the arm. "We graduate with a 3.44 GPA. Not too bad."

"Hardly a genius."

"Hey, it only goes to 4.0. And we're going to have to hold down a job while in college. Only so much time in a day for studying. And Kelly in the dorm room next to us is freakin' loud and obnoxious."

"I dunno. Why should I bust my ass like that?" 18-Sam shrugs. "College is for like snobby people who think they're smarter than everyone else. What's wrong with staying here, being an ordinary girl? My dreams are kinda stupid, actually."

"Dreams and ambitions are not stupid, but there's nothing wrong with being a small-town girl in general, either. However, it's not who I am. Or who you are. You want to help people. In fact, we end up being a federal agent."

18-Sam laughs.

A few people at tables nearby look over at her

the way people tend to look at those who randomly burst into laughter for no reason.

"Me? Working for the government? Dad would drop dead."

"He doesn't. Makes fun of us a lot, though. Can't say I've talked to them much since I moved out."

"Really?" She fidgets with a salt shaker. "That's sad. Why wouldn't you stay in touch with our parents?"

I gesture at her. "Because of stuff like the argument you just had. He called you dumb continuously for an hour. You understand how his mind works, right? We read books. He doesn't comprehend why anyone would do that, so to him, it's a waste of time. Anyone who reads is therefore lazy. Trust me, I know it hurt to have Dad call us a moron with no future over and over again. I lived this night, too."

She turns away from me. "Yeah, well... I have work to do, if you don't mind."

I watch my teen self head out from behind the counter and resume waitressing.

Dammit. I lean on the counter, kicking the toe of my sneaker at the floor. So bizarre being here again, looking out over the restaurant tables. Working here hadn't exactly been awesome, but what job really is? Mack is—maybe was, no idea if he's still alive—a pretty cool guy. Fifteen to eighteen had been a super complicated time in my life. I'd moved on from most of the kids I went to grade school who made fun of me for being the dirty hippie kid who didn't own shoes and didn't take showers. I did take showers, by the way. Just got dirty again real fast. Didn't help that our shower was outside the house in the backyard... a garden hose hanging on the wall with the brass nozzle adjusted to 'spray.'

We had an actual bathroom, but the shower broke and Dad never got around to fixing it... at least not until I was about fourteen.

So yeah, high school was a complex time of me trying to reinvent myself as a 'normal' person and not a wild, hippie feral child. Of course, some kids who knew me from grade school went to the same high school, but they didn't bother continuing to tease me. Freshman year, we'd all been mutually at the bottom of the totem pole, and by the next year I looked normal enough they left me alone.

Still, it's weird to see this place again. So many what-ifs. I could have ended up working here for a long damn time. Without my dream of becoming a federal agent, or at least going to college, I'd likely have ended up marrying someone I went to high school with and never leaving the area.

Wonder if I'd still be a vampire if that happened?

As I watch 18-Sam go from table to table, it starts to feel like she's giving up on college, letting Dad's words sink in and stick. I can practically see her body language changing from a smart, motivated teenager to an apathetic kid content to drift wherever the wind pushes her. Grr. What am I supposed to do here? Am I supposed to keep myself on course for the life I remember having? Or is the point of this merely to show me what might have happened?

I stare up at the stained ceiling above the counter. Can someone give me a sign if I'm dead? Is this the Origin? An alternate dimension? Or am I merely knocked so deeply unconscious I'm having messed up dreams?

A clatter of tinny bells accompanies the door opening. A late-twenties woman wearing a puffy denim jacket rushes in, red-faced and crying. She goes straight to an empty booth table, tosses her giant denim purse on it, and flops in the seat, head down, sobbing into her hands. Can't see her face behind her long, blonde hair, but I recognize her anyway. Only a few people I knew of around this time loved denim as much as Gwendolyn Pickett.

She's twenty-nine, has two small kids, and her husband's an idiot. I only know her because she showed up here three times a week for dinner for the two years I waited tables. Mack sometimes let her and the kids eat for free, and usually charged her less than he should have. They weren't poor, per se, but her husband Duane didn't let her have access to their bank account. Sometimes, they ran out of food in the house and he didn't seem to care. Control freak, big time.

Anyway, she often walked in crying but never quite this hard—except for one time, which I'm guessing is tonight. If memory serves, this is the night Duane left her. Which, all things considered, is totally an upgrade for her life.

Oh, shit. I get it now.

This night…

I'd been all bummed out after the argument with Dad, and just like 18-Sam, I'd been ready to give up on college and just cruise through life. Those tears 18-Sam wept earlier mourned the loss of the life she'd been dreaming about all year going up in smoke. Dad took a big ol' knife and stabbed it into my sense of self-worth.

The significance of this moment in time hits me.

Gwendolyn came in way more upset than usual. I remember talking to her as I often did when it got slow in here. Duane dumped her out of the blue. Picked up and took off for like New Orleans or some such thing. Left her with a part-time hairdresser job, a five-year-old, a three-year-old, and a little house she'd never be able to afford.

When I'd spoken with her tonight, she confided in me she thought about dropping her kids off at school in the morning then just going somewhere to kill herself. They'd be better off without her. Hearing a whammy like that had slapped me upside the head. Sure, I had problems with my dad, but they didn't seem so epic in comparison. I'd sat with her for two hours talking, got her through the worst of the sadness, and convinced her to fight for her kids' sake and not give up.

As a result of the conversation, I decided never to let myself end up like her—totally dependent on a man—and decided I'd go to college no matter what my parents thought about it. Talking to Gwendolyn also made me aware of how much I liked helping people. Probably had something to do with my eventual decision to pursue becoming a federal agent.

The two of us kinda saved each other that night… or this night, I suppose, since I'm apparently reliving it.

As far as I know, she found a lawyer in Crescent City willing to help her pro bono, since Duane took off without any official divorce. I half want to say she ended up marrying the lawyer a couple years later.

However, tonight, 18-Sam needs to have the conversation with Gwendolyn.

I tense up like I'm watching a horror movie loaded with jump scares as my teen self approaches her table.

"Hey, Gwen. What'cha havin' tonight?"

Gwendolyn keeps crying.

"Hey, if you need more time to think, I'll be back in a few."

What the heck?

I stare in disbelief as 18-Sam walks back across the place to the counter. She stops by the soda fountain, giving me this 'what?' stare.

"Aren't you going to talk to Gwen?"

"Umm, why would I? She's always crying. Totally bad vibes around her. Don't want her harshing my mellow."

I blink. "One, you're anything but mellow. Two, since when do you talk like Clayton?"

"What's that supposed to mean?"

"I mean, you don't say things like 'harshing my mellow.' *We* don't talk like that. We're not in a *Cheech & Chong* movie."

She rolls her eyes at me. "Whatever."

"Don't 'whatever' me, young lady."

"Don't 'young lady' me. You're not my mom."

"Mom wouldn't bother." I fold my arms. "And you're right. I'm not your mother. I'm you. I know exactly what's going on here and what's at stake if you screw this up."

She sighs. "Yeah, *whatever*. Clay probably just spiked my joint with LSD and you're totally a hallucination."

"Wouldn't that be nice? I'm not in your head."

18-Sam smirks at me. "Then explain why no one else in here can see or hear you?"

"No idea."

"If you're not a hallucination, what are you?"

"Still trying to work that out, quite honestly. I'm either you from an alternate dimension, you from the future, or I've just been killed and this is all some weird mind trip through significant moments in my life as, you know, the very core of my being slowly reintegrates into the Source of All Things."

"Whoa." She gawks at me. "What the hell did *you* smoke? Because I want some."

I sigh.

"No, seriously. Sounds like you got some great

shit. Could you give me a little?"

"Ugh." I facepalm. "Not high. Look at this."

Wings out.

18-Sam leans back. "Okay, maybe *I'm* the one on the good shit. Clay, you dork. If Dad finds out you got LSD—"

"He'll be pissed at him for not sharing," I say, frowning.

"Whoa." 18-Sam stares awestruck at me for a few seconds. "You *are* me."

"Yep. Now get over there and talk to Gwen."

"How about screw you and the wings you flew in on?"

I snicker. "Okay, that was a good one. But you have to talk to her and listen to her... and just be super kind to her."

"No, I don't. Like I said, Gwen's the physical embodiment of bad vibes."

"You've never talked to her?"

"Only to take her order. I think Mack's sweet on her, though." 18-Sam shrugs. "Why?"

"When I was your age working here, I used to chat with her every night. Yeah, she always came in upset, but that's because Duane treated her like crap."

"Who's Duane?"

I hang my head. "Wow, you really don't talk to her?"

"Nope."

"Okay, look. Duane's her husband. He's a jackass. Super controlling. Doesn't let her touch the bank account without permission or use credit cards. She has to ask permission to even spend money on groceries. She's got two kids, ages five and three, and tonight, Duane dumped her to move across the country. Gwen's so destroyed she's contemplating suicide. I talked her out of it back in the day."

"Go you," says 18-Sam.

I grab her shoulders. "What the hell is wrong with you?"

"Get off me." She shoves at me, but isn't strong enough to budge a vampire. "Whoa, what the hell?"

"I have big feathery wings but you're only freaking out that I'm stronger than you?"

"No, I'm freaking out that my acid trip is physically touching me."

"I'm not an acid trip." I let her go.

18-Sam snorts. "Which is exactly what every acid trip says."

Jimmy the cook rings the bell at the window slide. 18-Sam turns to grab the hot plates.

"Please talk to her," I say as she goes by. "You have to. It's about your future. Hers, too."

She 'pffs' and rolls her eyes.

The gesture is *so* Tammy it hurts. Or should I say Tammy is 'so me it hurts'?

I'm so grateful my kid grew out of the sarcastic know-it-all phase. Maybe I ought to be worried it hit her way earlier than eighteen. Doesn't matter. She's past it. Plus, my daughter had it pretty hard. Maybe not poverty-level hard, but she's 'seen some shit' as they say.

When 18-Sam returns after bringing the food to its table, she eye-rolls me again. "Are you still here?"

"Yep. I'm stuck here until you talk to Gwen and sort both of your lives out."

She leans a hip on the counter, crosses her arms. "And you know this how?"

"I'm guessing. There's not exactly a handbook for this." I tap my fingers on the counter, trying to think of something to say that'll convince her. "You were going to hang out with Pierce tonight, but you're in such a bad mood over what Dad said you're planning to go home and just go to sleep."

18-Sam ignores me, hurries off to help a customer.

But I'm not done with her yet. I chase her around from table to table, trying to say something, anything to get her to talk to Gwen. 18-Sam's gone into full 'screw it' mode and largely ignores me except for the occasional glare. One customer asks her if she's okay because she seems distracted. 18-Sam gives me this look like she's inches from screaming at me, but doesn't want to come off as crazy or get fired for being high on the job. She isn't, but she still thinks I'm an acid trip.

Vampire with angel wings who shapeshifts into a dragon? Maybe I *am* an acid trip.

Gwendolyn gets up, slings her purse over her shoulder, and trudges into the back toward the bathrooms. Oh, whew. Thought she was gonna leave.

18-Sam storms to the counter and slaps a ticket down in the kitchen window.

Jimmy asks her what's wrong and she starts bitching about our dad.

Bang.

Everyone in The Monarch falls silent at the gunshot from the bathroom.

Oh, shit!

We took too long.

I look down and sigh. A couple guys run down the hall and start battering at the door to the women's bathroom. Mack yells at them to chill out, he's got a key. He runs through me like a ghost… and the restaurant disintegrates...

Chapter Twelve
Trial and Error

I'm standing inside the doors of The Monarch.

Whew. Didn't permanently screw up. Like with the farmhouse exploding, whatever reality I'm in appears to reset if I get it wrong. Seriously, Elizabeth, why go to this trouble? Maybe she didn't mean to. Weird things can happen when dimensional energies are involved. Or maybe I really did get torn apart and I'm dead.

I clench my fists like a little kid eager to make the teacher happy.

Come on. I gotta get this right.

I walk over behind the counter. A minute later, 18-Sam emerges from the kitchen and stops short, staring at me.

"Hey, you can't be back here."

"Sure I can. I work here."

She gives me a fairly hostile 'who the hell are

you' up and down glare.

"Look, I'll be quick. I'm a future version of you, Samantha Radiance Sundance."

18-Sam raises both eyebrows. "Whoa. Clay must've spiked the joint with LSD."

"He didn't. Dad would get pissed if Clay did that."

"Who cares what Dad thinks? He's an asshole."

"Ninety-five percent agree with you, kiddo."

"You're not old enough to call me that. Besides, if you're me… it's kinda weird." 18-Sam walks out to check on the table with the ten-year-old boy. She returns carrying his empty soda glass to refill.

"I'm forty-seven."

"Bullshit."

"Thank you."

She glares at me. "What's that supposed to mean?"

"You don't believe my age. I'll take it as a compliment." I smile. "I know about the argument you had with Dad over school. You're going to spend all evening moping about it and feeling worthless. So bad you don't even want to go on the date with Pierce tonight. Well, dad's wrong. You do belong in college. In fact, you flourish in college."

Her hand shakes, but she keeps filling the soda. "What do you want?"

"You know Gwendolyn Pickett?"

"Bad vibes lady?"

"Yeah. You need to talk to her tonight. She's going to kill herself because Duane dumped her."

18-Sam turns away from the soda machine. "Be right back."

At least she didn't say "whatever." I stand there tapping my foot while she brings the boy his soda. She grabs the bills and check from an empty table and returns to the register, grumbling about bad tips.

"Duane's her husband," I continue. "He left her and she's going to legit kill herself. Tonight. Here. Right in The Monarch's bathroom."

"For real?"

"For real... unless you talk to her."

"Why the hell would I talk to her? I don't even know her." 18-Sam rings up the order and stuffs the $2.14 change into her tip pocket.

"Because in my reality, I talked to her all the time. We kinda became friends. She's really hurting tonight and needs someone to be there for her. It's going to benefit you as well."

"Does Mack make me clean up the mess?"

"Wow… Sam, what's wrong with you? I'm not this heartless."

"I'm not heartless. Just realistic. The world sucks. There's no reason to believe or dream or to even care. If I work my ass off to get a degree or wait tables for the rest of my life, my grave's gonna be the same size. Why put up with all the stress? It's stupid not to just peace out and let life carry me wherever it wants."

Our conversation rapidly degenerates into a long, roundabout argument. Eventually, I give up on getting her to talk to Gwendolyn (maybe it won't help if she's never spoken to her before, unlike me) and straight up try talking her into going to college. She sighs and rolls her eyes at all my fun college stories. She mocks me for wasting all that money to get nowhere in life.

"Hey, I went somewhere," I say.

"Yeah. Working for the feds."

"And eventually myself."

"Well, I think I'll just stay here for a while. Seems a lot easier." 18-Sam tromps off to respond to a guy in a cowboy hat waving at her for something.

Argh!

Before I know it, a gunshot comes from the bathroom. Oops, forgot about Gwen.

"Dammit!" I shout at the ceiling.

***

I'm standing inside the doors of The Monarch.

First thing I do this time is face the wall and smack my head into it. Argh! Damn. I owe Tammy an apology. She's *way* tamer than I was at this age. I barge into the kitchen, grab 18-Sam, and drag her out back onto the loading dock so she can scream all she wants. Also, my mind-control powers don't work on her. I can't do it to Tammy, Anthony, or Mary Lou either. I shouldn't be surprised I can't do it to myself. Heh. No self-control.

Argument number three rages until the gunshot happens inside.

Son of a bitch.

***

I'm standing inside the doors of The Monarch.

I stare down at my sneakers. Was I really this much of a bitch at eighteen, or is *this* reality making me worse? Okay, sure, I always did have a problem with dependency. Not on drugs, though. On people. Mary Lou mostly. Then Danny. It took me until like thirty before I really felt like I'd become a fully functioning adult, not a child needing the support of a real grown up. Finally working at HUD, pulling in a respectable salary, doing good for the community, yeah I'd fulfilled my goal. I had Danny, but I didn't end up *dependent* on a man to survive.

There's something here eluding me. Attacking it head-on isn't working.

Let me try sweet.

I wait for 18-Sam behind the counter. She walks out of the kitchen and stops short, staring at me.

"Hi, Sam," I begin, and rush an explanation of me being her from the future and attempt to sweet-talk her into helping Gwendolyn out.

"Sucks to be her, but why is it my problem?" Her vibes are like *way* dark."

"Because talking to her will save two lives today. Hers and yours."

18-Sam rolls her eyes. "Well, if it's so important, why don't you talk to her?"

I blink. Could it be that simple? Except only 18-

Sam reacted to me being here. Gwendolyn probably can't see me. Then again, she had her hair over her face when she walked in. She's fifteen minutes away from shooting herself in the mouth; she totally wasn't looking at anything around her. Holy shit. I remember that night we sat there and talked. I had no idea she had a damn gun *with her*. The way she spoke about suicide, she made it sound like a distant thought she kinda-sorta considered but wasn't really sure about.

"Guess it can't hurt to try. It's only our life hanging in the balance."

She gives me this 'you really need help' stare, shaking her head slightly, and walks off to check on tables. Mack goes by to meet the egg delivery. I step out from behind the counter and stand around watching the room, not bothering to pester my teen self for the fifteen or so minutes it takes before Gwendolyn Pickett walks in. Head down, she heads right to the empty booth, chucks her giant purse on the table, and flops in the seat.

I walk over and slide into the facing bench like I always used to do. "Hey, Gwen. You okay?"

"Oh, hey, Samantha. What's up?" She sniffles, swipes her hair off her face, and looks up.

Wow. I missed it as a teenager, but this woman *totally* looks ready to end it all. There's no life in her eyes.

"What'd the idiot do this time?" I ask while grabbing her purse and pulling it away from her, setting it on the bench to my left.

She stares at it. "Umm, what are you doing?"

"Giving you time to think and talk. I know what's in there."

Gwendolyn looks away like a child caught doing something bad.

Crap. I'm already off script. Did I screw it up already? What the hell did I say to her that night?

"Hey, this is the no judgment zone, remember?" I squeeze her hand. "Duane's a jerk and a control freak. It's not your fault. You should be thrilled he left."

She sniffles. "What am I going to do, Sam? He just took off. He's got all the credit cards. I've got no money."

"Hey, look at me."

Gwendolyn keeps staring off to the side.

"Gwen. I'm over here."

After a minute, she looks up, then squints at me. "You seem different."

"Yeah." I point at 18-Sam still standing behind the counter.

"Whoa, what the...?" Gwendolyn's mood shifts up a notch from fatalistic depression. "How are there two of you? And you look kinda... more my age."

"Long story. I've got two theories and I'm not sure which one is right. Either this is a parallel dimension where things aren't quite the same as my home world, or I'm dead and going through some life-reenactment stuff."

I explain my reality, how we met here when I

was a couple months from sixteen and we got to talking because she seemed sad, and so I had to talk to her—unlike 18-Sam who's wallowing in a haze of weed and self-pity. Or maybe not self-pity as much as she lacks any sense of self-worth since our dad destroyed it.

Gwendolyn cries the whole time I talk about how she'd come in here three or four times a week for food, and we'd always talk about life and stuff. It begins to make sense to me why she has a gun in her purse and is so damn close to ending it all tonight. 18-Sam hadn't befriended her, thus offering no outlet for Gwen. Everything had bottled up inside her, getting worse and worse until tonight. I bet *my* Gwendolyn in *my* world didn't have a gun in her purse that night. She hadn't been anywhere near as close to killing herself as this version of her.

18-Sam walks over looking like she's about to ask Gwen if she wants to order any food, but hesitates, standing there listening to me talk about our past conversations.

"You haven't had anyone to share this stuff with. In my reality, it had been me. That's why you're in the place you're at now. Please don't give up. It makes total sense to me why you feel the way you feel right now, but trust me. There are reasons to go on. You have three real big reasons to go on. Betsy, Austin, and Gwendolyn."

She sighs. "The kids will be better off in foster care."

"No they won't. They need their mother. Sure,

it's possible they could be more *comfortable*, have toys and stuff that you can't give them, but they won't have their mother."

18-Sam looks down.

"What happened to me in your reality?" asks Gwendolyn.

"You hadn't slid so deep into a black hole there, but I talked you out of what you were thinking of doing. You found a lawyer in Crescent City… wanna say his name was Jason something. Been a while, sorry if my memory's fuzzy. As far as I remember, he helped you officially divorce Duane, get half of the joint account, and custody of the kids. Not a huge achievement since Duane had no interest in being bothered with his kids again."

Gwendolyn scowls. "Yeah. He's not good with kids. Never wanted them."

18-Sam slides into the booth seat next to me. "Look, the first time you came in here, you were giving off all sorts of bad energy. Sorry I didn't talk to you or anything. I had my own problems to worry about, but maybe I should've said hi."

Gwendolyn shrugs. "It's okay. Who talks to complete strangers having a bad day?"

"Don't feel too bad." I pat 18-Sam on the shoulder. "It took me long enough to stop feeling like a kid hanging on everyone else for support."

"How long?" asks 18-Sam.

"I didn't feel like a functional adult until thirty. Mary Lou was there to hold my hand all the time and I never really let go of her out of some weird sort of fear. Probably because of our idiot parents."

18-Sam chuckles. "Yeah. Hi, Gwen. I'm Sam."

The three of us start talking, 18-Sam and I doing our best to convince Gwendolyn that Duane leaving is the best thing he could've done for her. Gradually, the sense of gloom lifts from her and the cloud of angst hanging over 18-Sam thins.

Right as it occurs to me it's weird no customers or Mack have approached us to complain about the place's only waitress hanging out at a table and ignoring everyone else, the room around me melts away to nothingness...

Chapter Thirteen
Detachment

The white glow fades to reveal my house in Fullerton.

I'm standing near the driveway by the detached garage, closer to it than the house. Nothing appears out of the ordinary at first glance. It seems I 'passed' whatever this weird situation required of me in The Monarch. Was the universe trying to show me how much of a difference I made? Or is Elizabeth simply trying to torment me?

Maybe none of this means anything at all and I'm having a weird dream.

Or a death experience.

Or maybe I really am in a padded cell somewhere, crazy as the day is bright.

Actually, I'm starting to think I *haven't* been destroyed. Going to the Origin is supposed to be all sorts of awesome and peaceful for the last little while before any sense of my ability to realize I exist is gone. Being thirty feet away from Gwendolyn blowing her own head off three times is the opposite of serene.

Okay, so here I am at my house; in particular, near the garage.

I always did hate the detached garage. Such a silly thing to bother me about the place I once considered our ideal dream home. We'd been so happy to buy this place, yet something about it having a detached garage always needled at me. Maybe scars from being teased as a child about how poor my family had been. Did I look at a detached garage as being lesser somehow? Guess I feared mockery for having the slightly lamer house.

Wood clatters inside the garage, then scraping like someone dragging a piece of furniture over concrete. I'm almost afraid to ask what to expect here, but standing around watching isn't the right answer. If I do nothing, whatever's going to happen will play out to its 'failure conclusion' and I'll reappear here again.

And again.

I walk around to the side facing the house and open the smaller 'person door.' A child's shocked gasp comes from the garage. Never a good sound. Kids only make that noise when they're caught doing something they shouldn't be doing. Worried, I hurry inside.

Tammy, all of ten years old, barefoot in a coral-colored dress, stands on Danny's old dresser in the middle of the garage. She's up on her toes, in the midst of tying a rope to a crossbeam in the roof. The other end of the rope is around her neck.

She freezes, staring at me. Her expression of being caught shifts to 'oh well, guess I'm in trouble.' Tammy lowers her arms from the beam, leaving the rope draped over it but not secure.

I rush over and grab her. Too gobsmacked to speak, I stand there holding her like a teddy bear, rocking her side to side. What kind of twisted effed up alternate reality is this? Holy shit. Elizabeth, if you made me see my daughter trying to kill herself at ten, you're going to die very slowly.

Tammy doesn't make a noise, squirm, or say a word, as if I'm holding a lifelike silicone doll made to look like her. Only her body heat and the motion of her breathing confirm she's alive. I don't remember the last time she wore a color other than black, grey, or purple. Probably around this age, actually. She didn't get really into the goth phase until like twelve. Guess having an undead mother got her interested in all things morbid.

"Sorry for making you cry," whispers Tammy.

Deep breath. "What are you doing, baby?"

"I wanna talk to Anthony."

Horrified, I hold her out to arms' length, staring into her eyes. "What?! Talk to Anthony?"

"Geez, ma. Why are you being so weird?"

Says the ten-year-old with a poorly tied noose around her neck. I set her on her feet, pop a claw, and slice the rope off her. Tammy goes bug eyed at the sight of my weaponized fingernail.

"Mom? What's happening?"

"Why are you in here trying to hurt yourself?" I ask. I pick the dresser up and move it back against the wall where it should be.

Again, Tammy gawks at me.

"Tam? What happened to Ant?"

She points at me. "You look younger. Did you get a face lift? Angie's mom got one, too."

"No, and it's kinda hard to explain. Where's Anthony?"

"With Daddy." She swishes side to side, making her dress flare a little.

"Why are you acting like you're six?" I brush a hand over her hair. Damn, her mind is still closed to me.

Tammy looks down. "Everyone's dead. Everyone dies. I'm gonna die, too. I miss Ant. Why are you being weird?"

I'm being weird? Oh, well… this Tammy doesn't know where I came from. Whatever version of me belongs in this reality would know the answers to the questions. "Dead?"

"Yeah. Are you pretending? I know you didn't forget."

"Tam Tam…" I wrap my arms around her, unable to help myself… and squeeze. Why is my kid acting like this? She's ten, but talking in the tone and cadence of a five-year-old, absent emotion.

"Tammy?" calls a voice sounding suspiciously like mine from the house. "Tams? Where'd you go?"

My daughter twists to peer at the garage door, making a WTF face.

"Hey!" shouts another version of me. "Get the hell away from my daughter."

I relax the hug and twist to look at myself. She's visibly older than me, a couple of grey hairs, too. Still wearing a HUD badge around her neck. Looks like she just got home from work. If Tammy's ten here, I'd be about thirty-seven… and this woman *looks* thirty-seven. Actually, she looks closer to forty-seven.

"What the fu—dge?" 37-Sam blinks at me.

"Hi, Sam. I'm you. It's weird, but I can explain. Before I do, you need to know Tammy was *this* close to hanging herself." I hold up the rope.

"What?" barks 37-Sam. "Tammy?"

The girl looks down, shrugs. "I wanted to talk to Ant."

37-Sam runs in and clamp-hugs Tammy.

Voices from the house tell me my sister's kids are over. They still sound relatively normal at least, though Billy Joe isn't shouting every word like he normally does. He's Tammy's age, so should be ten here, which means he ought to be the human version of a chihuahua strung out on caffeine. Limitless energy and limitless volume—only he's acting normal.

"Please don't," whispers 37-Sam. "I can't lose you, too."

"I'm going to die anyway," deadpans Tammy.

"If I die now as a kid, they won't make me get a job in Heaven."

"Heaven is just temporary," I say. "We go back around for another lifetime and won't remember the one before… unless we get stuck as a ghost."

37-Sam and 10-Tammy look at me like I attempted to speak Russian to them.

"Stop being a douchebag!" yells Ruby Grace from inside the house.

Neither 37-Sam nor 10-Tammy react much to the voices outside. But me hearing my sister's hyper-intelligent, shy eight-year-old swear like a sailor knocks my jaw open. I'm sensing unresolved anger issues not present in my reality. Oh, crap. What's happened here?

"So, Sam…" I offer a hand. "I'm Sam."

"So which one of you is my real mother?" asks Tammy.

"Both of us, though she is technically your mother more than I am here," I say. "Are you two aware of the weird stuff?"

"Weird stuff?" asks 37-Sam.

"Witchcraft, monsters, maybe vampires?"

"Oh." 37-Sam sighs, shrugs. "Yeah."

10-Tammy nods. "Yes. Aunt Mary Lou is a vampire. She's gonna kill me someday. I just know it."

"No, she's not," says 37-Sam in a tired sort of tone like she's had this argument over and over again.

"Wow. Elizabeth went for ML here, too?" I

whistle. "Interesting."

"You know about Elizabeth?" asks 37-Sam.

"Yeah."

"Stop being a bitch!" shouts Ellie Mae.

"Don't call me a bitch!" roars Ruby Grace.

"I wasn't talking to you!" yells Ellie Mae.

"Well, I can't be a bitch," says Billy Joe. "I'm a boy."

"You *are* a little bitch." Ellie Mae proceeds to say the word 'bitch' about fifty times before a meaty *thud* stops her.

Wail-crying follows.

"Aunt Sam!" chimes Ruby Grace from a window in the house. "Billy Joe just hit Ellie Mae!"

37-Sam and I exchange a 'she kinda deserved it' look before she puts on her 'Mom face' and storms out of the garage, crosses the yard, and enters the house. I follow. What? I live here, too. 10-Tammy and I stand in the kitchen watching as 37-Sam yells at Ellie Mae for teasing her brother, him for hitting her, and Ruby Grace for using bad words. My alternate self attempts to bargain by offering not to consider them in trouble if they calm down and be human beings for the rest of the day.

Surprisingly, the kids settle in and get absorbed in television.

37-Sam trudges back into the kitchen with a 'shoot me' face on.

I have no choice but to hug her in sympathy.

"So what's going on here?" she asks me.

Since she knows about vampires, I figure she

can handle what I have to say. So, I explain about dimensions, focusing mostly on the idea of lateral third-dimensional worlds. Some are vastly different —like with dragons and stuff—while others are only slightly altered from the reality I consider mine. "So, I'm either from one of those other realities and landed here somehow or I'm being absorbed by the Origin of All Life. Or maybe it's a dream. I'm kinda leaning toward the idea of Elizabeth randomly flinging me into an alternate reality, but that wouldn't explain why I've been stuck in *Groundhog Day* scenarios which reset if I screw up."

"Damn. And I thought my life was rough." 37-Sam opens the fridge and grabs a bottle of red wine.

"Already? It's only five," I say.

"Five is late for her." 10-Tammy shrugs. "Mom's usually tipsy by now."

37-Sam looks away, pissed, but doesn't bite Tammy's head off. The kid didn't mean it as an insult. Children are brutal with the truth.

"Let's talk…" I sit at the kitchen table.

10-Tammy tries to wander off, but I snag her and pull her into my lap like a teddy bear. She doesn't seem thrilled but tolerates it.

37-Sam sits, glass of wine in front of her.

We talk, and I learn in this reality, Elizabeth took Mary Lou instead of me, only a few years later. Ruby Grace hadn't even been born yet in my world when I became a vampire; here, she was about a year old when Elizabeth took her mother.

Ever since ML turned, this Sam has been taking care of her kids. Rick, ML's husband, is still around, but he works long hours and isn't home as much as he'd like to be. He and 37-Sam have kind of a swap shift arrangement going with all the kids. When she's at HUD, Rick has kid detail. She picks them up from day care on her way home and keeps them until morning.

Her telling me Anthony died at age seven rips my heart out and gets 10-Tammy crying… and thumb sucking. Oh, no. She's shattered. Great, now I'm crying too. It shouldn't surprise me they lost Anthony in this reality. 37-Sam not being a vampire would mean she never had access to the ruby medallion, nor the ability to make anyone else into a vampire. Apparently, Mary Lou didn't think to do it, wasn't around, or the 'UPS driver' never showed up with the medallion at all. Would this world's version of Jeffcock have been involved if Elizabeth went after my sister?

37-Sam goes on to tell me how Danny couldn't handle the grief of losing Anthony. He started drinking heavily, lost his law practice, and started managing a 'nightclub.' 37-Sam wags her eyebrows along with the word nightclub. I nod in a 'yeah, I know' manner. She means the strip club in Colton but doesn't want to say it in front of our daughter.

"Seven months ago, Danny was in a car accident coming home from that place. He'd been drinking. Swerved into oncoming traffic." 37-Sam looks down.

They say carrying a grudge is unhealthy. However, Zen isn't my thing. I'm *still* so irritated at Danny for what he did to me vis-à-vis the kids that hearing he killed himself doesn't faze me in the least. Tammy squirms, cuddling up in my lap, acting way younger than she is.

Dammit 37-Sam, what are you doing? This girl needs to be in freakin' therapy. She's not only borderline suicidal, she's regressed. I say 'borderline' because she wasn't trying to kill herself specifically because she wanted to die, merely because she thought she'd become a ghost and be able to talk to her brother and father.

"You look shocked," says 37-Sam. "How did it go in your reality?"

"A lot different." I give a sad chuckle. "Elizabeth got me instead of Mary Lou."

Tammy shivers, pulls her thumb out of her mouth, and stares up at me in pure terror.

"I'm not a vampire anymore, sweetie. I got better." I take her hand and put it on my cheek. "See? I'm warm. Not gonna hurt you."

She relaxes, mostly, then resumes sucking her thumb. I gingerly pull her hand away from her mouth and hold her close while mouthing 'therapist, now' at 37-Sam.

She looks, down, guiltily. "Yeah, I know. Just… barely making ends meet as it is."

"Been there."

I talk a bit about how things went in my universe. Tammy snaps out of her daze at my explanation of Anthony's weird existence. 37-Sam isn't sure if she prefers it to his being gone and reincarnating.

"Does Mary Lou visit?" I ask.

"No, not really. I haven't seen her since the night she figured out she'd become a vampire." 37-Sam drains the last of her wine. "It's kinda weird she hasn't made contact."

"Maybe it's for the best."

"Yeah, probably. I think she doesn't trust herself not to be a danger to us." She glances at the fridge, but decides against more wine.

"Or she's grumpy because she can't drink booze anymore."

37-Sam chuckles. "She liked her margaritas."

"And wine coolers," I say. "Gotta hand it to her, though. She never got *drunk*."

"Mary Lou is tough."

"Except when it comes to horror movies," I say. "If you talk to her again, tell her Elizabeth is lying. Mary Lou doesn't *have* to contain her. The bitch is messing with her. Our sister is not the only thing standing between her and the end of the world."

"Really?" 37-Sam brightens a little.

"Yeah." I explain the whole Red Rider situation. "Just tell ML the bastard hurts kids and she'll hunt him down, too."

"Like you did?"

"Yeah."

She nods. "Hey, can I ask you something?"

"Sure."

"It's about Mary Lou's husband, Rick."

"Um, okay."

"With Danny gone and Mary Lou pretty much out of the picture... things are getting kind of interesting between us."

I raise an eyebrow. "You're wondering if the two of you should back off or start a relationship?"

Tammy looks up. "I want Daddy back."

37-Sam fidgets. "Something like that."

"Well, it's actually impossible for Mary Lou and Rick to be together romantically. Any mortal who becomes involved with a vampire ends up losing control of themselves and becoming a mental slave. Danny and I got lucky. He couldn't bear to touch me afterward due to certain temperature issues."

37-Sam squirms.

"Rick's a nice guy," I say, shrugging. "You're both alone. Um, I think you guys could be good for each other."

"Wow. Wasn't expecting you to say that." 37-Sam tries to drink from her empty glass, sighs, then puts it down. "Been holding off on going anywhere with it for now. I don't want to make life worse for Tammy."

"You and Rick getting together isn't replacing Danny."

"He... seems to really care for me. For us."

I poke my daughter in the side, almost getting a half-smile out of her. "Your Uncle Rick is a good man. I think your daddy would want someone like him to be there for you."

Tammy replies with an 'I guess so' one-shoulder shrug.

Hmm. I get it. I'm here because I used to ask myself all the time if everyone around me would have been better off if I'd never been made a vampire. If Elizabeth chose my sister instead of me, she'd have destroyed two families instead of only mine. And she didn't totally destroy mine, only changed it. Would we have been better off if it never happened to me? It appears not. *This* is freakin' heartbreaking.

Poor Anthony.

I peer into Tammy's eyes, trying to insert a mental compulsion never to harm herself.

Alas, it's like banging my face into a stone wall. Still doesn't work on family.

I scoot my chair back, stand with Tammy in my arms, and relocate her to 37-Sam's lap, pushing them together in a hug.

"Sam," I say. "Please get her some help. Tammy is in a bad place now. I think if you're comfortable considering a relationship with Rick, it's probably the right thing for you. I always trust my gut. If your gut's saying go for it, then listen."

37-Sam wraps her arms around Tammy. "I'll try, but it's overwhelming."

"Oh, here." I grab a paper from the counter and write down Allison's phone number. "Call Allison Lopez. In my reality, we're kind of best friends. She's a psychic. Maybe she can help talk to Tammy and settle her demons. Not sure if she's going to believe the dimension stuff right away. In my reality, we experienced it together so I didn't have to convince her. If she doubts you met me, mention Millicent the ghost. The three of us were members of a triad of witches in past lifetimes. I'm sure she'll sense the connection to you."

"Umm… weird, but okay. I guess I'll try anything if it'll help Tammy."

I pluck my daughter's hand away from her mouth. "Tam Tam. Please stop. You'll mess up your teeth."

She gives me this 'so what if I have bad teeth, I'm going to die soon' stare.

I bow my head, eyes closed, drowning in guilt. No. I totally do not wish it didn't happen to me. I accept my reality. I'm even happy about it. Please let this Tammy find help.

She's always been way more sensitive than she admits.

"Hey, Moon!" shouts Nico Fortunato… my old boss at HUD.

I open my eyes to find myself standing in the office, two desks away from my spot. Nico doesn't seem to be talking to me, but the occupant of my cubicle.

Ugh. Now what?

Chapter Fourteen
Stoner Kid

Tammy stares at the soldiers surrounding her, knives poised.

Heart racing, she spins, searching for a way out. Mom and Elizabeth zoom back and forth so damn fast she loses track of where they'd even gone. Kingsley growls somewhere in the dark. Allison's fireballs shoot overhead like flares. The man who'd grabbed her from behind and dragged her off lay on the ground not far away, cradling his groin, but his friends catch up to her before she can get back to the Light Warriors.

A man in front of her grins, raising his knife. *"Tiempo de morir, puta."*

Tammy knows two or three of the words. *Die* and *bitch*.

She scrambles back, but another man is behind her, also with a knife.

Tammy does the only thing she can think of to protect herself—projected a telepathic scream far louder than any sound her vocal cords could produce. The soldiers surrounding her recoil, grabbing their heads. She keeps picturing the shriek in her mind, trying to make it louder, deafening, brain-numbing.

And that's when an explosion hits her in a white blur.

She braces for pain... but nothing hurts.

When she stops cringing, she opens her eyes to a familiar street. Somehow, she'd ended up back in Fullerton, three houses away from home at the end of the cul-de-sac. Her mind fills with hundreds of voices all talking at the same time. She winces at the barrage, but at least with so many, she doesn't hear anything particularly disturbing. The worst part about her 'gift' is picking up on people thinking *super* creepy stuff, like wanting to hurt people... or worse.

She quickly fetches the faerie amulet from her pocket, puts it on.

The world falls quiet... as quiet as it ought to be to a normal person. Only the tweets of birds, a distant lawn mower buzzing, and a few distant—actual—voices reach her ears.

Tammy twists around, blinking. How the hell did she get here? Did that bitch blast her all the way back to California?

The neighborhood looks normal, except for it being daytime. Late afternoon from the look of it. It had been night in the forest.

Bewildered, Tammy follows the curving side-walk home, feeling a bit like a kid in gym class who took a dodgeball to the face one too many times. At the chain link fence surrounding her house, she stops short.

"What the...?"

The grass is as high as her waist. Beyond, one of the living room windows has a trash bag over it, covering a gaping hole in the glass. The rain gutter on the right side of the house is drooping. The garage itself is literally tilting to the left like it might collapse at any moment.

Mom's van is missing, but Dad's old BMW sits in the driveway. The car *looked* nice, but broke down more often than guests on Dr. Phil. Looks were everything for a struggling attorney, and pulling up in a BMW gave off the illusion of success. Or so Dad believed.

Except, of course... Dad had died years ago.

Somewhat more than a little freaked out, Tammy turns right up the driveway and heads to the metal gate in the fence. Beyond, the cement path leading to the front door overflows with grass. She stops, staring. Maybe whatever Elizabeth did somehow sent her back in time. A voodoo spell had sent Mom back in time.

Cautiously, she unlatches the gate, steps through, closes it behind her.

A spot of metallic blue in the grass to her left gives her pause. As she gets closer, she recognizes it as Anthony's bicycle, the same one he got for his seventh birthday. It lays on its side near the house, nearly hidden in the grass and weeds as if it had been sitting there for years. The chain had turned entirely to rust, as had the pedals, though the tires had little wear as though the bike hadn't been used much at all.

Huh? Ant rode the heck out of that bike. Why is it even here? Dad gave it away when Ant outgrew it.

"Get outta my room!" shrieks a girl inside the house.

"Again?" barks Dad. "I told you not to let me find this shit in the house."

"So stop looking for it," says the girl.

"That's not how this works, Tammy. You're out of control and that's scaring me."

Tammy slow blinked. *Wait. Is that me?*

She ditches the bike and hurries around the house and through the side gate. She follows the shouting to her bedroom window, where she climbs up onto the central air unit and peeks inside.

Dad, completely alive and *not* a dark master, stands in the doorway, even more disheveled than she remembers. His suits had always been like the BMW, old but well taken care of. But this man in front of her looks like a Wall Street banker who'd been living homeless on the street for a week. Unshaven, messy hair, loose tie, stains on his suit, shirt unbuttoned, but worse of all—he appeared *broken.*

Her room also doesn't seem quite right either. Some of her posters were in the right place, but all the lighter stuff has disappeared, replaced with posters and images from death metal bands she didn't really like all that much as their music went way too dark.

The bed, other than having black sheets and comforter, look the same except for one huge difference: *another* Tammy sits on it. She appears younger, maybe fourteen, hair chopped to shoulder length. Seeing it so short makes Tammy grab her hair protectively.

Impostor Tammy rocks black lipstick, heavy eyeliner, a spiked collar, ripped T-shirt with an up-side down cross on it, black mini-skirt, fishnets, and Frankenstein boots with three-inch platform soles. She also wears handcuffs, both ends locked around her left wrist like a bracelet.

Tammy gawks at herself, noting all the eye shadow in the world can't hide the red glow of being high. This kid looks like one of the stoners the school resource officers tended to follow down the hallways and randomly frisk for drugs or weapons.

What the hell is going on?

She glances at her father and dives into his head. He'd found a baggie of weed—again—in younger Tammy's room. He's freaking out with worry that she might be starting on harder drugs like heroin. The words 'where did I lose her' repeats on a loop in his thoughts, blurry as they are under a haze of alcohol. *Oh, wow, he's drunk or close to it.* Unfortunately, he can't think of anything else to say, afraid everything he might try will get thrown back in his face by a daughter who hates him for no reason he understands.

"Seriously?" snaps the younger version of herself. "You of all people are getting on me about weed?"

"Tammy..."

"Tell you what, why don't you just go pour another fucking drink and give me back what's mine."

As her disheveled dad shakes his head, looking for all the world like he could use a drink, Tammy shifts her attention to her younger self.

The other girl has no resistance to her telepathy, nor apparently any psychic powers at all. Concentrating on the idea of 'why are you like this,' she digs past the immediate sense of anger and resentment at her dad barging into her room and searching it for drugs. Someone named Robby McKee would be pissed at her for losing the weed. Beneath that lay a boiling rage at the world in general. 14-Tammy hates existence. She'd given up caring about anything beyond enjoying herself in the moment. She thought of her dad as an irritating failure for always trying to get in the way of her having a good time. He couldn't do anything right. Shitty lawyer, shittier pimp. He still practiced law on the rare occasion he got a client, but mostly he co-owned a strip club with some creep.

Shockingly, every other word in 14-Tammy's thoughts are curse words.

Tammy squeezes the windowsill, trying not to make a sound under the barrage of pain and rage now filling her head. Still, she dives deeper. Dad's more of an asshole in the morning when he hasn't been drinking. Thinks he's some kind of perfect role model and authority on what's 'bad' or 'good.' As if the man didn't sell women at night. Yeah, he didn't know she knew his 'dancers' worked as prostitutes off the books. 14-Tammy had lost all respect for her father once she figured out he basically managed a brothel. Even if the women were technically not 'supposed to do that,' her father did nothing to stop them and got a cut of the take. The idea they broke the rules by hooking existed as a legal technicality only to protect the club.

Below that, she sees memories of Anthony's funeral when he'd been seven years old. He'd died of some mysterious illness the doctors couldn't even figure out, much less cure. He'd gone from happily running around the soccer field one day to dead in a single week. And Mom wasn't at the funeral.

What? How?

Older memories distort and twist into nightmarish forms. Whoa. Tammy backs out of her younger self's thoughts and attacks her father's mind with the focus of 'what happened to Mom?'

In his head, she watches him receive a call at his law office. Nico Fortunato tells him his wife was killed during a drug interdiction event. Her mother had been shot and killed.

Tammy gasps. The tremendous crush of grief in her father's memory breaks her concentration and snaps her out of his head.

No! That's totally wrong! What the hell is going on? Yeah, Mom got shot, but she didn't die. I was only four... but I remember it.

She wipes tears off her face, thinking about how Mom got stuck couch surfing for a while as she recuperated. Despite wearing a bulletproof vest, she'd suffered a pretty nasty injury that left her sore and unable to move around too well for a few weeks.

But she survived.

Gathering her composure, Tammy thrusts herself into Dad's mind again, digging for answers. Mom didn't like bulletproof vests. Oh, crap. Apparently, she hated wearing them, and her father figured she decided not to wear one that day as she expected to stand around doing nothing while the FBI took the lead.

She gathers still more information...

This Tammy had been kicked out of three different schools for setting fires. Almost went to juvie for getting caught with a knife in the hallway. Wait. What about Mary Lou? Why didn't she step in and help?

The answer lay in her father's memory. Mary Lou disappeared without a trace a year before her parents bumped into each other. Danny had never met her. Aunt Mary Lou hadn't married Rick. Her cousins didn't exist at all.

Where the hell am I? Why is everything so messed up?

"Tammy, please," says Dad. "The only thing I want is for you to be okay."

This can't possibly be real. She had to be stuck in a nightmare or something. The white energy bomb Elizabeth set off must have knocked her out.

"Who fucking cares?" 14-Tammy says. "We're all gonna die. Maybe tomorrow. Maybe a year from now. It could happen any time." She gets up and stands before him—then snatches the bag of weed out of his hands. "So I might as well have a little fun until it happens."

She storms off, flipping him the bird.

Dad slouches, every ounce of his body language awash in defeat.

From the window, Tammy watches him, confused by her own emotions. Ever since he'd tried to separate her and Anthony from Mom—and flat out lied to them, claiming Mom didn't want them—Tammy hadn't been too fond of her father. That said, it hurt seeing him look so broken.

He sits on the edge of Tammy's bed and wept into his hands. His thoughts leap to Mom's funeral. In it, four-year-old Tammy watches the casket being lowered into the earth and asks him, "Daddy, how long does Mommy gotta stay down there?" After he stops sobbing too hard to speak, he tells his little girl that Mommy doesn't need her body anymore, that she's in Heaven.

"What happened to my little girl?" whispers Dad now.

Heartbroken, Tammy curls up on the central air fan and cries as well.

Amid a flash of light, Tammy finds herself standing on the street again. In fact, in the exact spot she'd appeared earlier. "What the crap?"

She looks up at the blue sky and perfect clouds. Fullerton mocks her with its tranquility, the exact opposite of the storm inside her house. Still reeling from watching Dad's memory of her mother's funeral, Tammy doesn't even try to stop herself from sobbing.

That is, until a car drives right through her and pulls into the driveway next door.

"Holy shit!" Tammy stumbles, falls.

Their neighbor, George, had hit her dead on, but his car had passed through her like a ghost vehicle. Tammy finds her feet, rakes her hand through her hair.

"This is so messed up. What the hell is going on?"

14-Tammy and Dad start shouting at each other again. She can hear them even from a few houses away. No point going around back and peeking in the window again; sounds like they're repeating the same lines as before.

This time, Tammy stops at the corner of the yard. She can't bear to watch the scene play out again. Mom hates it when she or Anthony uses coarse language, yet this version of Tammy curses like a sailor. The girl probably did it on purpose to break rules. If Mom died when she'd been four, she wouldn't understand her mother hated bad words. Or at least wanted her kids to turn eighteen first before using them.

Even though she could 'legally' swear now, Tammy doesn't feel much need to do so unless something serious happens—like a demon trying to eat her. Trivial everyday stuff no longer rose to the level of needing extreme language.

Hmm. Maybe I'm supposed to try helping this Tammy? Maybe I can tell her Mom wouldn't like her swearing? If she chills out even a little, Dad and younger me might get along better.

Tammy swallows the giant lump in her throat. It had been there ever since she saw that both Anthony *and* Mom were dead. But, this can't be real, right? It must be some kind of nightmare. But how could she escape it? Or *could* she escape? Then again, she might only be stuck until she wakes up.

Wake up, wake up!

So far, no such luck.

Meanwhile, 14-Tammy storms out the front door, slams it, and tromps down the walking path to the gate at the driveway. The girl appears stuck at a teetering point between furious and wanting to cry. Finally, she nods, opens the gate and heads to the sidewalk. There, she hangs a right, turning away from her older self, not seeing her.

Tammy follows the girl, nervous about being

seen.

After a few blocks, 14-Tammy abruptly whirls around. “Hey! Are you following me?”

“Umm...”

14-Tammy blinks, the aggression in her fading. “Whoa, trippy. You kinda look familiar.”

Tammy walks closer so they don’t have to shout at each other. Compared to the younger girl’s over-the-top goth outfit, Tammy’s black T-shirt, ordinary jeans, and sneakers make her feel like a norm. Since turning eighteen, she’d been chilling out on the morbidity stuff lately. “This is going to sound really weird.”

“I like weird,” says 14-Tammy. “Do I know you?”

“Kinda. I’m... you… at eighteen.”

“Aww shit. You mean I go lame?”

Tammy shrugs, both offended and amused. “I guess. I never really got as into the goth thing as you are.”

“Wow.” 14-Tammy whistles. “Julio must’ve given me some primo shit this time.”

“I’m not a hallucination.”

“Yeah, sure.” 14-Tammy rolls her eyes and resumes walking. “Every hallucination would say that.”

Tammy falls in step beside herself. “Can I ask you something?”

“Sure, LSD trip, go ahead.”

“Why do you and Dad fight so much?”

“He’s a hypocrite and a liar and, well, a terrible

parent. Oh, and he owns a fucking strip club. He's been lying to me about it forever."

"Do you blame him for lying about it?"

"Yes. No. Whatever. It's embarrassing."

"Do your friends know about it?"

"No! I would seriously die if my friends found out."

Icky subject. Tammy decides to talk about something else. "In my world, Mom didn't die in a drug raid. She had a bulletproof vest on. Only broke a couple ribs."

"Bullshit," snaps 14-Tammy. "Mom wasn't wearing a vest because Dad said she never did any real dangerous stuff. She was supposed to make sure cheaters didn't get the cheap houses. So, screw you."

14-Tammy picks up her pace.

Tammy jogs after her. "Wait… aren't you even curious why we have different memories?"

"Nope," mutters 14-Tammy, not slowing down.

Tammy bites her lip, continues following the younger version of herself for several blocks until they arrive at a seemingly abandoned house. It totally looks like a drug den from some James Franco movie, the sort of place Tammy would never go near. Except 14-Tammy goes straight in the door, no hesitation at all.

Her stomach knotted in fear, Tammy stands at the spot where the sidewalk and walkway intersect, trying to work up the courage to go into a 'crack house.' She didn't know they existed so close to her home in Fullerton.

"This is a dream. I can't really be hurt, right?"

Jaw clenched, she heads up the walkway to the porch. She moved over to a window and peeks inside.

14-Tammy, along with a blue-haired girl and three guys, sit around on furniture abandoned here no doubt by the previous owner. All of them appear to be high-school-aged. Trash, mostly pizza boxes, beer cans, and snack chip bags, cover the floor, coffee table, mantel, and TV stand. Most everyone has a beer in hand, including young Tammy. The oldest boy, however, drinks from a smaller bottle concealed in a paper bag. Only 14-Tammy reacts to her watching them through the window, giving her a dismissive 'screw off' eye roll. Then proceeds to ignore her.

"Hey, Tam," says a Hispanic kid in a black hoodie. "You wanna try some blow?"

"Blow? This isn't the damn eighties, Julio," says 14-Tammy.

He shrugs. "Whatever. Do you want some or not?"

"Yeah, why not? Screw it."

"No!" yells Tammy. She tries to beat on the glass... and falls through it harmlessly, without a sound.

14-Tammy's eyes bug out at the sight.

The older boy swipes the glass coffee table clean. Julio dumps out a tiny packet of white powder. Tammy runs over and tries to kick the coffee table over, but her foot passes through it like a ghost's. Blowing on the drugs doesn't help either. 14-Tammy laughs at her futile attempt to interfere.

When her younger self leans over to snort the coke, Tammy grabs at her—getting a solid grip. She drags 14-Tammy away from the table. The girl kicks, flails, and shouts at her to get off.

The other kids all stare at her.

"Whoa, Tam, I think you already had too much," says the oldest.

"You give her the funny weed, Julio?" asks the other girl.

"Nah. Just normal stuff. But the girl just flew across the room. You all saw that, right? Ain't no drug gonna do that unless we are *all* trippin'."

Meanwhile, 14-Tammy elbows her hard in the stomach. "Get off me!"

Tammy doubles over, collapsing to all fours, gasping.

The younger version of her tromps back to the table. "Hey! Which one of you assholes took my line?"

No one admits to it.

"You guys suck." 14-Tammy flops to sit on the floor and glares at Tammy from across the room. "Thanks for that."

"You're welcome," rasps Tammy. "What's wrong with you, anyway? We're not into drugs."

"You're clearly lame."

"Who's lame?" asks the other girl in the room.

14-Tammy says, "Not you, Indigo. *Her*."

Three sets of eyes turn to Tammy... but don't focus on her. No surprise. Tammy's pretty sure no one but her younger self can see her.

"There's no one there," says Indigo.

"Whatcha seeing, Tam?" asks the older boy. "A ghost?"

"I'm seeing myself, but I'm older... and I'm seriously lame." 14-Tammy mimics an overly innocent voice. "We don't do drugs. We're good girls."

The others laugh, though still seem a bit confused.

Tammy walks over to her. "Mom would be heartbroken if she could see you like this."

14-Tammy jumps to her feet. Considering the platform boots, she actually stands a little taller than Tammy. "No one says shit about my mother."

"Chill out," says Tammy. "We have different memories. There's gotta be a reason for it. My mom didn't die when I was four. She doesn't let me swear, either. It really bothers her. Why don't you relax with the bad language... for Mom."

"You sound just like our asshole dad."

"He's a mess, but he loves you. He just can't show it."

14-Tammy snorts. "Then maybe he should stop drinking all the time and be real. And maybe ditch his, um, second source of income."

Tammy knows she's talking about the strip club. "I agree. On both counts."

"Damn," whispers Julio. "She's high as shit. Or

am I? You guys seeing this?"

"Girl got issues," says Indigo.

Tammy ignores the others. "Dad dies in my reality."

"I should be so lucky," mutters 14-Tammy.

"You don't mean that."

14-Tammy shrugs. "How'd he die?"

"It's a really, really long story."

She narrows her eyes. "Then summarize."

Tammy exhales. "Hold on, lemme think. Okay, Mom got turned into a vampire. Dad couldn't handle it. He went a bit crazy. Got into black magic thinking he might be able to 'fix' Mom, but he got killed by another vampire who was trying to kill Mom."

14-Tammy blinks, mouth open. Then spins to face the room. "Wow. I am astoundingly fucked up. I'm so high my hallucination is tripping balls. What did you give me, Julio? How the hell can I even still walk?"

"Just weed, Tam. Blue lightning. Nothing fancy." The boy shrugs innocently.

"He's not lying," says Tammy. "And I'm not a hallucination."

Young Tammy shakes her head. "I need to get out of here. You guys coming?" She doesn't wait for an answer and storms outside.

The others exchange glances, shrug, and follow.

"Dammit," mutters Tammy.

She falls in with the group, though only 14-Tammy could see her or touch her. If she tries to grab any of the other kids, her fingers pass through them. As they walk, the group tosses around ideas for how to have fun. As they do, Tammy keeps trying to convince her younger self to go home and talk to Dad, but the girl ignores her. Desperate, she starts telling her about how Anthony doesn't die, either, in her reality because their vampire mother turned him into a vampire too, but then gave him his soul back with a medallion. Now he's got the ability to turn into a giant fiery warrior. 14-Tammy laughs, believing herself to be on the wildest trip ever.

Lonnie, one of the sixteen-year-olds, gets the idea to steal a car and joyride it.

Everyone except Indigo loves the idea.

"No way, guys. I got nailed for shoplifting last month. If they pick me up in a stolen car, I'm done. If you guys are seriously gonna do that, I'm out." She holds her hands up.

"No worries, girl." The oldest, Robby McKee, high-fives her. "We got this. Catch ya later."

The group moves on the down street, minus Indigo.

Tammy keeps pace with her younger self, speaking as she walks. "You really need to bail on this, too."

14-Tammy holds up her middle finger without looking at her. "You can go away now, LSD trip."

Tammy sighs and follows the group. Eventually, Robby finds an older muscle car that he manages to break into. The others act cool while he crawls under the steering wheel and messes with some wires. As soon as the engine starts, they all pile in.

"Nope." Tammy grabs her younger self, dragging her back.

14-Tammy again elbows her in the stomach, knocking the wind out of her. When Tammy stumbles away, cradling her stomach, the younger version of herself jumps into the back seat. Gasping, Tammy scrambles after the car, diving through the closed door like a spirit. She grabs hold of 14-Tammy and hangs on for dear life.

The car burns rubber and lurches into the street.

Tammy clings to her younger self despite the girl pushing, punching, and shoving at her. Once she pulls her foot in out of the floor, the car abruptly becomes solid around her. She lets go of her angry young self, not at all happy to be sitting in the back seat of a stolen car.

Dreaming. This is a twisted, messed up dream. Why am I having this dream? I've never *done anything like this. Not even close.*

Meanwhile, 14-Tammy cheers and whoops at Robby's erratic, fast driving.

She's going to end up dead or in jail before she's sixteen. Tammy's heart sinks. *Is that what she wants? Or is this all to hurt Dad?*

"Tell him to stop!" shouts Tammy, loud enough to cut through the din.

"Piss off."

"Please, let's get out and go home. You really need to talk to Dad. Trust me, okay? I'm you. I know what's best."

"You know nothing, lame-o," says 14-Tammy.

Flashing blue and red lights erupt behind them.

Tammy twists to peer out the back window. "Oh, crap."

"Police!" yells Julio.

14-Tammy starts to give the cop a double middle finger, but Tammy grabs her arms and pulls them down.

"Such a bitch!"

The cop turns on his siren once it becomes clear the kids won't pull over. Robby takes a hard left turn while running a red light, nearly creaming a guy on a motorcycle.

Tammy screams in terror. "Stop the car, you idiot! Pull the hell over!"

Except the boy can't hear her.

Tires squeal. Robby swerves from lane to lane, doing ninety on a four-lane street downtown. More police cars come out of nowhere, something like eight or nine of them following in a train.

"Jesus, he's gonna get us killed," says Tammy. "Tell him to stop."

"My lame hallucination thinks you should stop the car and let the cops get us," says 14-Tammy. "She's afraid we're gonna crash."

"With my mad driving skills, never." Robby laughs and speeds up. "Plus, this thing's got a monster engine. I can outrun the cops, especially on the freeway where I can really open this thing up."

Laughing, 14-Tammy crawls over Lonnie's lap.

She leans out the window up to her waist, and waves at the police following them. Probably flipping them off, too.

Tammy grabs her younger self's legs, struggling to pull her back into the car.

"Shit!" yells Robby, yanking the wheel, making a rapid lane change left to avoid a box truck at a complete stop in the road. Except they veer into oncoming traffic.

As they zoom past the truck, 14-Tammy's body jerks, along with a loud *whump.*

Tammy's eyes widen in horror as the girl goes limp over the door, no longer supporting her own weight. Time appears to freeze. She didn't want to look at what happened to her younger self.

Directly in front of them, a garbage truck rapidly approaches.

Tammy closes her eyes, waiting for the boom.

***

No explosion.

Instead, she finds herself in the cul-de-sac, a few houses away from her home.

"I'm stuck," she says, tears in her eyes. "Like in a video game or something."

Worse. I'm stuck somewhere Mom doesn't even exist. Mom...

She sits in the middle of the road, wraps her arms around her legs, and sobs.

"Mom… please help me. Where are you?"

A few minutes later, 14-Tammy storms out of the house.

Tammy looks up at her younger self. "Here we go again."

Seeing her alive again lights a fire under her, getting her moving up to a sprint. As soon as she catches up, she grabs her younger self by the hand.

"Hey!" shouts the kid, spinning into a defensive posture. "Whoa, what the hell?"

"Tammy, listen to me, you can't go hang out with those losers or you're going to die."

"Did my dad pay you to say that?"

Tammy takes in some air, tries a different tactic. "Mom sent me."

14-Tammy grabs her by the shirt collar. "Say another thing about my mom and I'm gonna—"

"Hear me out!" yells Tammy. "I am you four years from now."

"Trippy." She lets go. "Okay, if you're supposed to be me from the future, how can I die now? If I do, you won't exist."

"Alternate dimensions."

"Gimme a break."

"Will you get over yourself for one damn second and think?" shouts Tammy. "Look at me! We are the same person. You're so preoccupied with being pissed off at everything and everyone, you aren't even paying attention to what's going on around you. Do you want to die?"

14-Tammy scowls. "No. I'm not suicidal. I just don't care."

"Not caring if you die isn't much different. Look, I totally know how you feel. I'd be so messed up if something bad happened to Mom… something kinda bad did happen to her, but she's different in my reality. I know you still love her. I don't understand why you are acting like this. If Mom saw you here, it would break her heart."

"Good!" yells 14-Tammy, her eyes puffy, brimming with rage and tears. She shouts so hard her voice fries every few words. "Serves her right for having such a stupid, dangerous job. Why did she have to go play around with guns and get shot? Why'd she have to get herself killed?"

"You're angry at her."

14-Tammy turns away. "Of course I am!"

"I… I was too for a while. I was kinda little when it happened to her, so I didn't understand. It's different in my reality, though. She didn't get killed on her job. She did something real stupid and went out jogging at night."

"Wow. That's dumb."

"Maybe not. Mom said she thinks it would've happened anyway, even if she didn't go jogging. Probably true. The thing that attacked her would have come looking for her no matter where she was at the time. If she'd been home, it might've killed me and Anthony."

"You're not making sense anymore." 14-Tammy folds her arms.

"When I was four, my mother got turned into a vampire."

Young Tammy waves dismissively. "You're crazy. I don't have time for this."

"You've taken goth into 'trying too hard' territory, but you don't think vampires are real?"

14-Tammy flips her off. "I'm goth, not an idiot. That stuff doesn't exist."

"You're trying to be edgy because you're so angry at everything. Yeah, I'm totally with you on Dad needing to quit the strip club. You really could get him to quit, you know. If you promise you'll knock it off with the drugs if he quits the club, he'd totally do it."

"How the hell do you know that?" 14-Tammy spins to glare at her again.

"I'm telepathic. Being around a vampire mom for fourteen years did something to me. I can read your mind."

"Really? What am I thinking?"

"I'm completely crazy and you want me to go away."

"Duh. That doesn't take mind reading to figure out." 14-Tammy laughs.

"Think of something embarrassing you'd never tell anyone." Tammy blinks. "Whoa, you made out with Lucy Stafford?"

14-Tammy storms off.

"Hey, not judging. Just caught me off guard you actually did it," yells Tammy, running to catch up.

"I'm not gay. I was high as hell," grumbles 14-Tammy. "If you tell anyone, I will cut you."

"I *can't* tell anyone. You're the only one who

can see me here."

"Oh, duh. Of course you know about Lucy. You're a hallucination coming from my brain. Nice try with the psychic thing. You had me going there for a bit."

"Stop."

"No."

"Please?"

"Go away." 14-Tammy keeps walking.

Tammy sighs. True, she'd been a little mad at her parents for being idiots. She'd gone through a rebellious period, pretending to be aloof. Inside, she dreaded something horrible would happen to Mom and she'd be alone. Even at her worst, however, she never lashed out like this girl. But, she had Mom. This girl didn't. Is this how she'd have ended up if Mom listened to Danny and left? She wouldn't have been around to save Anthony, wouldn't have been involved in her life. She'd been way closer to Mom than she let herself admit.

What am I supposed to be doing here? What's the point of this? Is it a video game or is it a nightmare?

She follows 14-Tammy to the same crack house. Rather than pull her away from the cocaine this time, Tammy continuously tells her Mom would cry if she saw her snorting drugs. The nagging works. 14-Tammy passes on the coke, claiming her Dad would send her to 'a place' if he caught her taking anything worse than weed.

Before long, the idea of going to do something

fun comes up. Tammy hurries after the group, trying to talk 14-Tammy out of going with them. When Indigo bails on the car theft, Tammy tells her younger self how Mom would feel about joyriding a stolen car… but the girl merely gets angry and keeps going.

Tammy literally shakes in panic at the idea of sitting beside her younger self as she's killed by a box truck again. Would this Dad have to go identify the body? Did they even ask people to identify decapitated bodies? She nearly throws up at the thought. Robby climbs into the car and gets to work hotwiring it.

No.

Tammy grabs her younger self, dragging her away from the car before it starts, determined to get her so far away from the damn thing, the others would leave without her.

"Get off me!" yells 14-Tammy.

"No! You're going to die if you get in that car. You're gonna die really bad, too." She continues fighting to drag her along.

A few people walking down the street gawk at 14-Tammy, who to them must have appeared to be sliding mysteriously.

14-Tammy flails, trying to grab onto a sign post. "No one tells me what to do. Not my dad, not LSD hallucinations. And I don't care if I die."

"Yeah, well, Dad cares." Tammy's grip slides up on the younger girl's baggy T-shirt.

"You're gonna rip my damn clothes off. Stop!"

Tammy hauls her younger self around, putting herself between the girl and the car. They've gone almost a block away, so she feels reasonably safe letting go. "You can't get in that car. Robby's going to drive like an idiot. The police are going to chase them, and he's going to crash head-on into a giant garbage truck. Everyone in that car is going to die."

14-Tammy scrambles to her feet. "Yeah, so what? At least then I'd be with Mom and Ant instead of a father who just wishes I'd die, too. Then he wouldn't have to hide me from his sleazy—"

"Stop!" yells Tammy. "Dad doesn't want you to die. He's home crying right now, wondering what happened to his little girl."

"You're so full of shit." 14-Tammy scoffs. "You're not even real. You're like my guilty conscience or something. I don't have a conscience anymore. You died when Mom did. Go away."

"No. Mom wouldn't want you throwing your life away."

"Stop talking about her! I told you!" roars 14-Tammy before leaping into a punch.

Tammy catches her arm. Alas, the goddess Freya no longer empowered her with the heart of a warrior. Fortunately, an enraged fourteen-year-old high on pot didn't fight anywhere near as well as ancient Nordic zombies. Despite taking a few elbows in sensitive spots and a hair pull, the fight ends in a minute or so after she drags the scrawny girl to the ground and sits on top of her, pinning her to the sidewalk.

"Get off me!" yells 14-Tammy.

"Not until you promise not to get in that car."

"Screw you."

"Think about Mom, okay? What would she want you to do?"

14-Tammy spits at her.

"Gah!" Tammy wipes her face.

14-Tammy yanks a switchblade off her boot, snaps the blade out, and stabs Tammy in the gut. "Get off me, bitch!"

Tammy wails in pain, clutching the wound. 14-Tammy shoves her aside, yanks the knife out, and runs off. The thud of a car door follows a moment later, then the screech of peeling tires. Gasping, Tammy looks down at her stomach. Blood rolls out of her belly, dribbling onto the sidewalk. It hurts too much for her to move. No one walking by notices her there.

She curls up in a ball.

A small packet of pills lay on the sidewalk in front of her face, likely fallen out of 14-Tammy's pocket during the brawl.

Is this real? Would I really have gone so crazy if Mom died? Where am I? Is this a lie?

The stab wound throbs like a hot iron poker stuck into her belly.

Ugh. What's happening?

In about fifteen minutes, the car would crash, killing them all. Tammy would reappear on the street again. She doesn't know what to do. 14-Tammy has gone so far off the deep end, she seems beyond saving. No wonder Dad is a wreck.

Am I going to be stuck here forever, doing this over and over? I want to wake up from this nightmare.

She closes her eyes.

Mommy... Where are you? I need help.

Chapter Fifteen
Worked Too Hard

I probably should have expected to end up in the HUD office at some point.

All right. Let me think. What in the ever-loving heck is going on? Did Elizabeth destroy me and I'm having a twisted 'this is your life' flashback thing?

Hmm. I'm going to say no. No peacefulness at all. And those sort of precious moments things only exist in Hallmark movies. Also, if such a recap really did happen, I'd be watching it, not having to make decisions and do things about it.

Am I skipping around alternate dimensions? Possible. It is more than a little coincidental, however, for me to keep landing in times and places relevant to my life. If I am playing alternate dimension hopscotch, there is some force at work sending me to specific places. Could be whatever 'big white explosion' magic Elizabeth did is responsible for this.

"Sam?" calls Nico.

"Sec," yells Sam from my desk.

It doesn't even surprise me now to hear myself speaking when it's not me speaking. Obviously, I'm here because it's me.

"Oh, hello, Sam," says Ernie Montoya—to *actual* me.

I turn to peer behind me. The agent who mentored me is standing in the aisle close by, looking right at me. He's still wearing the pink shirt with white collar and cuffs, but he's not the Ernie I remember. His hair's gone grey and he's gained about fifteen pounds.

"You can see me?"

"Only for a moment," says Ernie in a voice that doesn't belong to him. It's deep, resonant, and fills me with a tingly sense of warmth.

I blink in disbelief. "Azrael?"

Ernie nods once.

"Why did you possess Ernie?"

"I didn't. I merely look like him. He's still at his desk."

I peer over at where Ernie sits, and notice the entire room around us has paused in time. Even the coffee dripping out of the samovar into Bryce's cup has frozen like an icicle. "Are you really here or part of the weirdness?"

Ernie smiles. "I'm here. But only for a moment. I've a simple message."

"Okay."

"You've been catapulted into a dimensional non-space. These realities you are seeing are taken from alternate dimensions closely matched to yours. Your body remains elsewhere while your soul is being thrown around by Elizabeth's magic. She is attempting to break you down."

"Why?"

"Quite simply, Elizabeth is trying to distract you with grief to keep you stuck in an eternity prison."

"So she *didn't* kill me."

"No."

"Then how do I get out of here?"

"The same way you've been doing. It is an elaborate puzzle box."

I growl. "Never liked escape rooms. Being trapped pisses me off. Hate it."

"I know."

"What brought you here?"

"I've merely come to tell you the truth about your situation to help you focus."

"Thanks." I exhale. "Good to know she didn't destroy me. What about the others?"

"Having similar experiences."

"Wait, she threw us *all* into this place?"

Ernie nods again. "Yes."

"Are my kids okay?"

"If you mean alive, yes. Your daughter will not escape her prison. Your son will. The others will also fail."

"What happens if they don't escape?" I breathe into my hands to stay calm. What's happening to

Tammy?

"They will simply remain trapped in the alternate dimension, repeating the same experiences over and over again until released from the outside."

"You mean, until I help them escape?"

"Exactly."

I exhale. "Okay. So how much longer am I stuck here?"

"That is up to you, Sam."

And with that, Ernie/Azrael disappears.

Crap. Okay. I got this.

A pale—obviously vampire—version of me slathered in sunblock gets up from her desk and walks to Nico's office. Through the glass wall of his office, I can see that his tone and body language suggests he's about to yell at an agent for screwing up big time. Sam slides through the door and sits before him, arms crossed. They begin speaking, quietly at first—until Nico goes a little red in the face. And now he's full on yelling. Others in the office look over. Wow, this Sam must have messed up big-time.

But within seconds of Nico starting to bellow at her, he goes quiet. Inside the office, Sam cracks her neck, then casually gets up and saunters out, leaving Nico sitting at his desk, gazing into space.

Oh, Sam. What are you doing? Ugh!

HUD-Sam stops a few paces from her cubicle, staring at me. "Do I even want to know what's happening?"

I walk up to her, grimacing at the overwhelming scent of coconut.

"Short answer, I'm you from an alternate reality."

"Um... what are you doing here?"

I smile. "Trying to find the way back to where I belong."

"Not here to mess with me?"

"Nope. Elizabeth's a bitch. She threw me into a dimensional Wheel of Misfortune. Are you still containing the bitch?"

"Yeah. Got a tight lid on her." HUD-Sam tilts her head. "Why? Did you let her out?"

"Kinda sorta. 'Let' isn't exactly true, but she got out. It's not a big deal. But she's been lying. We're not fated to spend the rest of eternity shielding the world from her. Not saying you should let her take you over, but go ahead and kill the Red Rider if you get the chance."

"The what?" HUD-Sam blinks.

"Forget it. He might not even exist in this reality."

"Sam? Who are you talking to?" asks a younger man I don't recognize. He's maybe thirty, Hispanic, short hair.

HUD-Sam looks at him. "No one. Sit down."

He goes glassy-eyed and mechanically obeys.

"Are you mind-controlling everyone in the office?" I ask, eyebrows up.

"I have to. Not proud of myself for it, but it's the only way to make this job work."

I glance at the Hispanic guy—who's sitting at Chad's desk. "Did Helling transfer to the FBI?"

"No, he's dead," says Sam in a fairly heartless tone. "Nico kept sending us out into the field. This guy got the drop on me. Shot me in the chest. Chad tried to play hero, but it got him killed." She gestures at the Hispanic guy she just told to sit down. "That's Alonso. He's my fourth partner."

"Fourth? Wow. Do I want to know what happened to the other two?"

She shrugs. "They died, too. It's why I decided to stop letting Nico send me out into the field during the day. The sun is murder on my reaction time and perception. You still working with Chad in your—what did you call it—alternate dimension?"

"No. I made a real mess of a prisoner escort soon after Nico reinstated me. Decided it would be safer for everyone for me to resign."

HUD-Sam makes a face like I'd suggested throwing babies into a bonfire. "After everything we went through to get here, and you just quit?"

"I didn't want anyone to get killed because of me."

She looks down. Regret's a bigger bitch than Elizabeth… only this Sam doesn't seem too broken up by it. More like a 'yeah, that probably would've been a better idea' face. "Interesting. I couldn't give up what I worked for. Once I figured out I could *make* people do things, keeping my job was easy."

"At what cost?" I whisper.

"A couple people died. So what? The world's

got plenty."

"Whoa. You're not talking like, well... me."

She shrugs one shoulder, steps into her cubicle, and sits. "Maybe my lid on Elizabeth isn't as tight as I think. We talk now and then."

"Oh, crap. You let her out, didn't you?" I enter the cubicle area and pace in the little area behind the chair.

"Maybe a little. And no, I'm not evil, if that's what you're thinking. I don't hurt anyone… well, not anymore. Worst thing I do is pull a salary a little higher than I ought to for sitting at a desk crunching numbers and running audits all day."

"Just so you can still claim to be a federal agent?"

"I *am* a federal agent," says HUD-Sam. "No one, not even Elizabeth, is taking that away from me."

Hmm. "Let me guess. Danny's at home, enthralled to you?"

She grins. "No. He wouldn't touch me."

"Same. My Danny couldn't even look at me."

"Did you kill yours?"

I gasp. "No. Of course not… but he did die."

"Ooh, how?"

"Tried messing with dark magic thinking he could cure me. Got betrayed by another vampire who wanted me dead. He ended up turning into a sad excuse for a dark master."

HUD-Sam laughs. "Idiot. If you're curious, mine tried to take the kids away from me. Do you believe he told me I'd only be 'allowed' to have fifteen minutes on the phone with Tammy and Anthony once a week?"

"Yep. Pulled the same crap with me."

"Who the hell did he think he was talking to? He clearly failed to comprehend the difference between mortals and vampires. Hunters and prey."

"Oh, no... you didn't." I stare at her in horror.

"Oh, I did. As soon as it got dark, I went straight to his parents' house. Twisted Danny's head right off his neck. Threw it at his obnoxious parents, then removed them from the gene pool as well."

"Holy shit…" I sink to sit on the second chair, no longer able to stand. "I can't… what about the kids?"

"Oh, they're fine. Both were asleep. They think Danny hooked up with a blonde bimbo from his strip club and moved to Florida."

"Doesn't Tammy know?"

HUD-Sam narrows her eyes at me. "Why would she?"

"Because she's phenomenally psychic from being so close to Elizabeth for so long."

"Not sure it worked out the same way here, hon." HUD-Sam shrugs. "Did you seriously manage to keep Elizabeth totally contained?"

"As far as I know, yes… at least until she escaped."

"Maybe it's like a pressure cooker. She tried so hard to overwhelm you, the energy she threw off affected your Tammy. My daughter is a perfect angel." HUD-Sam points at photos on her desk.

Anthony and Tammy look like the kids of some rich corporate type in nice clothes, smiling broadly… except Anthony doesn't appear older than seven in any of the pictures. Tammy, despite wearing nice dresses, about as un-goth and mainstream as possible has this 'someone please help me' stare in every picture. Obvious fear/concern in her eyes gets worse and worse in each successively older photo. The oldest she appears to be in these photos is about eighteen. One image shows her alone, wearing a Cambridge University sweatshirt. In that picture, she looks calm.

Holy shit. My daughter had to leave the country to feel safe. Anthony's obviously a vampire, too. How did he show up in the pictures? Make-up?

I feel a little sick to my stomach. My poor baby boy...

"Okay, this makes no sense why I came back here." I rub my eyes, scanning the familiar office. Azrael said this entire thing is Elizabeth trying to mess with me. She must be hoping to hurt me by making me see such horrible things I can't do anything to fix. Not sure what she's going for though. *This* is exactly why I resigned from HUD. Her putting me in this situation is only confirming I did the right thing. The worst part about this 'world' is thinking about the lives my kids had here. Tammy looks like a kidnapper is holding a gun to her head in every picture—except the college one—forcing her to 'smile.' I can't surrender to my emotions.

Must get out of here. *My* Tammy needs me. Anthony's strong. He can protect himself much better than she can. "I moved on from here."

"Maybe you did, but I couldn't. You know how much work went into getting this job."

"I do. And, I also know the harm it would have caused to stay here. I had to leave."

HUD-Sam cocks an eyebrow, smiling like a succubus. "Did you though? Did you really let it go?"

I purse my lips, thinking. Is this 'scenario' Elizabeth trying to mess with me or am I really still carrying baggage about this place? Chad's dead. And two other people are dead because of me. This entire department reduced to mind-control puppets…

"Yes. As a matter of fact, I did let it go. Sure, I grieved having to give up being a federal agent, but look at all the harm it's caused to stay. I made the right choice. I'm sure of it."

"Hmm." HUD-Sam examines her severely pointy fingernails. "Interesting."

"And I know this is not coming from inside my head. This office, you, everything around me is *not* my guilt talking, because I don't have any guilt for quitting HUD. This is Elizabeth screwing with me."

The office around me disappears.

I'm standing in a plain white void again.

I stare up into the nothingness.

"Okay, what now?"

Chapter Sixteen
Judgment

The last time I had this much blank nothingness staring at me, I'd been giving a presentation about HUD to a bunch of high school students.

It hadn't so much been them wanting to send the new girl—I'd been on the job three months at the time—but Ernie enjoyed doing those career day events and he was my mentor. Hmm. Am I done or is the universe having problems loading the next dimension?

An exit would be nice.

But no...

A large residential dining room decorated in a style of anal-retentive grandmother appears around me. I'm standing a few feet away from the narrow end of a rectangular table. Danny's mother sits at the opposite end facing me. Another Sam sits at the midpoint of the long side on my left, Danny opposite her. Danny's dad is sitting directly in front of actual me, his back to me. I think I'm about twenty-four in this moment. We'd been married not quite a year. Tammy would be three years in our future.

24-Sam stares down at her plate, seemingly avoiding eye contact with an enormous painting of Jesus on the wall behind Danny. He would tell me later that Jesus didn't normally live on that wall. His mother temporarily hung it there so he would stare at me.

Modern me would have blithely made a quip asking her if she normally hung it in her bedroom to keep Mr. Moon off her. Modern me doesn't beat around the bush.

I am reminded again that for the first few years of our marriage, Danny had been under his mother's skirt. Whatever she wanted, happened—with the exception of him leaving me. He's hung in there... for as long as he could. I'm still not sure how he found the spine to resist her on that.

Mrs. Moon didn't think I was good enough for her Danny. My family had zero money and less status. I'd have told her my father once played minor league baseball but it wouldn't have helped. Probably made it worse. Even major league, she'd have sneered at, sports being 'barbarian activities' and so on.

Danny's parents acted like multi-millionaires even though they weren't.

Not only had her precious little boy gotten involved with a dirty hippie, I had a 'maybe later' reaction to their religion. All it took was one 'not really' to her asking me if I attended church and I made a mortal enemy forever. At the time, I didn't have any negative feelings about religion whatsoever. She just kinda made me dislike it. Though, to be fair, I more disliked *her* than the actual concept of it.

Wow, would it fry her brain if she found out I'm working for an angel? I should totally go visit them and reveal my wings. Nah. That would be evil and just as petty as hanging a giant portrait of Jesus to stare awkwardly at your son's new wife during dinner.

Though, I had no doubt Jesus existed. In fact, I'm kind of surprised I hadn't run into him yet.

Anyway, despite me standing in clear view of the table, no one—not even 24-Sam—appears to notice me.

"I don't think this is going to work, Daniel," says Mrs. Moon suddenly. "This girl of yours is not right with God."

Grr. Watching me sit there like this passive little demure thing, hands folded in my lap, staring down, pisses me off. Come on, young Sam, grow a damn backbone. Of course, it only pisses me off because it's exactly what I did. As a kid, I ran from confrontation. I used to randomly run like hell away from adults sometimes if they looked too much like cops, important people, or creeps even if they had no interest in whatever mischief I did. Usually, I wound up hiding behind Mary Lou. As a teen, I casually walked away from most conflict. Granted, by then I no longer stole vegetables or did mischief. In my young twenties, I tried being quiet and invisible, and hoped no one noticed me.

Later, my federal training would help me find a backbone. Even a HUD agent isn't a great job for people who hate conflict. I still don't enjoy conflict, but I've discovered the ability to—I don't want to say 'thrive' on it—endure. Well, more than endure. Nowadays, conflict gives me an adrenaline charge somewhere between exciting and 'let's not do that again.' I'd much rather spend my days keeping my kids safe, watching *Judge Judy*, and doing casual background checks. But I'm no longer afraid of conflict.

And I definitely wouldn't sit there like a servant girl while the old crone talks crap about me right to my face. Oh, by the way, I stopped looking like a 'dirty hippie' at around fifteen. Mrs. Moon merely heard I grew up 'rural' in NoCal and made assumptions. It didn't make it hurt less she'd basically been right. Any family where everyone routinely smokes weed and clothing is more of a 'feel like it sometimes' situation rather than a requirement is honestly hippie. Except for my brother Clayton, we all grew out of the random nudity thing in our teens. Mary Lou had been the least into weed, probably because she preferred wine. I only gave up the weed when I decided to join HUD. They kinda frown on that.

"I'm not sure what we're doing here," says Mrs.

Moon. “Daniel, you should do the right thing and find a proper girl.”

“Ma, you’re not being fair,” says Danny, not looking at either of us.

“Listen to your mother, Daniel,” mumbles Mr. Moon. He always sounded like he kept half an ice cube in his mouth and talked while trying not to spit it out. “You can do better.”

24-Sam cringes, head bowed, as if afraid to make a sound.

Oh, hell no. This is giving off *Handmaid’s Tale* vibes way too strong. Was I that pathetic?

Ooh, just seeing them talk about me like I’m not even there… telling him to divorce me right in front of me. Hey, this is a ‘video game’ right? If I mess up, it merely resets. No one really gets hurt in video games…

I extend my claws.

***

I reappear in the Moons’ living room at the end of the table.

Okay, so doing violent things to Danny’s parents was *not* the correct answer. So, yeah, I can mark that off the list. Sadly, it didn’t really make me feel better, even if I’d daydreamed about it for years.

When the scenario resets, it feels like the Jesus painting is staring at *me* more than at 24-Sam. Okay, fine. I won’t slaughter Danny’s sanctimonious, judgmental parents. Really wasn't at all fulfilling. HUD-Sam, who in all probability gave in to Elizabeth, would have adored it. Well, duh. She *did* kill them in her reality. I'm guessing her obsessive need to cling to the job gave Liz the opening necessary to get her claws in, an opening I never gave her.

In hindsight, what would have happened if she took me over? Would 'riding' me like a car up into the higher dimensions, bask in the detonation of the Red Rider, and crawl out of my throat as her physical body formed even have been necessary? Something tells me my experience with the immortal witch killer would have ended much differently if she'd taken control of me earlier. Either I'd have become entirely Elizabeth and my soul would've disappeared, or I'd have somehow died as she tore herself out of me.

Ick. Whatever.

The Moons start talking about me like I'm not in front of them, berating my lack of social standing, money, manners, and of course, faith. 24-Sam tolerates it for a little more than half an hour before she stands up and storms out of the room, going all the way out of the house to the curb. Mrs. Moon smiles as if she won.

At least I had stomped out. That was something.

I remember the night. It's exactly what I did. Had my love for Danny not been as strong as it was, our marriage would have ended due to the verbal tirade brewing inside me. Storming out hadn't been me no longer able to tolerate hearing Mrs. Moon rip on me. No, I left so I *didn't* rip back. The things swirling around my head would've made the Jesus painting spontaneously combust if they flew out of my mouth. Danny would have been so stunned at me excoriating his parents right in front of him he'd probably have caved in to their pressure and ended the marriage. He really did love me a great deal, but if my becoming a vampire later was too much for him, telling his parents exactly what I thought of them now would have been, too.

Still at the table, Danny doesn't quite scold his parents for being nasty to me. More like hinting they were out of line than saying so. My husband keeps gently asking them to try a different approach, to give me time, and 'perhaps be a little more polite.'

Mrs. Moon accuses Danny of being impolite by bringing a 'godless hippie' into her home.

Grr. I can't take her anymore.

Killing her has failed in this reality. I can't talk to her—they are unable to see or hear me—so the only reasonable thing for me to do is leave the house like my other self. She's standing by the curb, arms folded, regretting going outside without her coat. I think this happened in early December. Not Christmas dinner, which had been another nightmare scenario.

Anyway, 24-Sam mutters to herself, debating a life spent with the toxic in-laws from hell. Our marriage hadn't even reached the one-year mark, and she's thinking of giving the parents what they want and agreeing to separate. She's pissed at Danny for not defending her in front of his parents. I was, too. Still am. The man never could contradict his mother in front of her. He always stayed quiet. If memory serves, around the time Tammy was three, I hit Mrs. Moon with an 'if I wanted your opinion, I'd have asked for it.' Her reaction would've been appropriate for me throwing cat poop on her dress. She *really* didn't like me talking back to her. She liked it even less when I gave her a taste of her own medicine and spoke to Danny about her while she stood right beside us, saying things about how his poor mother was off her meds, needed constant care, and had delusions of being important and wealthy.

Go figure, they didn't want me around after that. Surprisingly, Danny finally found the nerve to defy them and refused to go to their house for social events without me. Thus, my kids rarely saw the Moon grandparents… well, until Danny basically abducted them.

Anyway…

The night I'm observing now, I remember stewing on the sidewalk for a while to calm down, then going back inside once the urge to verbally rip Mrs. Moon's face off subsided. I hated how Danny and I could be so perfect and in love at home, yet the minute we went anywhere near his parents, we couldn't even function or look at each other.

In hindsight, it's not surprising Danny cracked

under the strain of me being a vampire. He believed I had died, and I'd been the island to which he clung to escape his domineering mother. Nah. If he really wanted to escape her, he wouldn't have invited her over to help keep me away when he stole the kids from me, forcing me out of our house.

Whoa. Okay, not how I remember it. Real-me went back inside after convincing myself 'marriage required some sacrifices.'

"Sam?" I start after her. "Where are you going?"

She stops, twisting to respond, but the sight of me leaves her visibly shocked.

"Don't be alarmed," I say. "I'm here to help."

"W-who are you?"

I smile. "Think of me as your guardian angel. You're upset at Danny for not defending you in front of his parents, and you have every right to be. But running isn't the answer. Come on, we haven't done that since Rebecca Milson got on our case in eighth grade."

24-Sam scowls. "Ooh. I hated her."

"I know. No idea why kids whose parents are well off think they're better than kids whose parents have nothing. Not like Rebecca worked for any of it."

"Seriously," mutters 24-Sam. "So, why are you here? Am I about to die or something?"

"Nah. You're about to make a mistake that will prevent our children from coming into being."

"I have kids with Danny?" 24-Sam gawks at

me. "We really last that long?"

"You do." I ramble about the kids for a little while, reminding her how wonderful it is to share life with Danny when his parents aren't around. It's tempting to say he loves us so much it totally broke him when he thought we died, but no point giving this version of me nightmares. Things have been so damn different in some of these alternate dimensions, it's possible she isn't destined for vampiredom at all.

"So what should I do?" asks 24-Sam.

"What do you want to do?"

"Grab that old bitch by her hair and bang her face into the table a few times."

I chuckle. "Trust me, it's completely unfulfilling. How about you ask Danny to stand up for you? Seriously, he's just sitting there letting his parents tear us apart and not even trying to stop them."

24-Sam glares at nothing in particular. "Yeah. You're right."

"If nothing else, Danny should defend us."

"Absolutely!" says 24-Sam.

She storms back into the house.

I follow, fingers crossed.

"Oh, you're back?" asks Mrs. Moon in a disdainful tone. "I thought you'd returned to your hovel in the forest."

Danny gives 24-Sam the same 'I'm sorry' look he gave me when I returned. Only, I quietly sat down and proceeded to ignore the derision for the remainder of the night. Later, at home, I told Danny never to bring me there again… a request he wouldn't be able to keep until I alienated the Moons by talking about them as if they'd gone senile.

24-Sam goes around to his side of the table and takes his hand. "Danny, I know how much you love me. It isn't right that you are sitting here letting your parents say all these bad things about me and not defending me. It's almost like you *want* me to leave."

"No!" He breaks out in a sweat. "That's not true. I just…"

"Are you going to let her talk to you like that?" asks Mr. Moon.

Danny twitches, face reddening. "Like what, exactly, Dad? She's only asking me a question. You and Mom *have* been a little condescending toward her."

A little? I raise both eyebrows.

"It wouldn't be a concern if you found a proper girl," says Mrs. Moon.

"Mom, she *is* proper. Sam is a federal agent. I don't think it's…" He hesitates. Looks 24-Sam in the eye, and seems to find courage. "I don't think it's right for you to keep insulting her like this. She is my wife, and if you have any respect for me, you will respect my choice of who I married."

Mrs. Moon gasps, hand over her chest.

"Don't you dare talk to your mother like that," barks Mr. Moon.

"Like what? I'm only asking her to be polite." Danny points at him, eyes going slightly wild.

Uh oh. He's gone into his lawyer mode. The hyperkinetic way he gets when in court. It's almost like he sets Danny Moon aside and becomes a character. Part Jim Carrey, part Scarface. I wince as he flies into a tirade like he's shredding a witness in front of a jury, only in this case the jury is 24-Sam and the shredding is aimed at his parents. He points out their false high-society act, that they've only got eighty grand in the bank but act like millionaires. He moves on to attack their hypocritical religious views, calling them out for acting in various hateful ways completely in contradiction to the beliefs they claim to hold.

The Moons get heated, screaming back at him. Lots of 'how dare you' flying around. 24-Sam gets in on it as well, defending Danny from the parents. For a few chaotic minutes, it feels like I'm standing on the set of one of those crazy reality shows where people damn near get into knock-down fights. Right as it seems as if silverware's going to go flying, Mrs. Moon abruptly changes tactics and starts fake crying, screaming at the ceiling and asking God why he gave her such an ungrateful, awful son. She moans about 'all she did' for him and this is how he pays her back.

The situation rapidly disintegrates.

Danny shifts from attack to cleanup, apologizing for upsetting her. She twists it around, saying this fight proves that 24-Sam is evil and trying to turn him against his own family and mother. And… like the spineless piece of crapola

Danny proved himself to be later in life, he caves in.

Divorce court, here they come.

Worse, 24-Sam is fuming. “Well, good. I thought I married a *man*. Not a little boy who lives under his mother’s skirt!”

She storms off a second time, walking right through me like I’m a ghost.

Crap!

In a brief flash, everything resets. 24-Sam is once again demurely sitting at the table absorbing verbal derision.

Well, I suppose this is why I didn’t insist Danny defend me that night. Perhaps part of me knew how it would end. He really had been deep under his mother’s skirt back then, afraid to face the world on his own.

When the time comes, I’ll try convincing 24-Sam to go back inside and simply tune her out.

Maybe that will work.

Chapter Seventeen
The Eternity Prison

Although it hurts watching 24-Sam flinch at Mrs. Moon's snide remarks, convincing my younger self to endure this trial either proved to be the right answer or broke reality, apparently.

Time freezes. A noise like shattering glass comes from above and to my left. Black jagged cracks race across the wall, widening until large sections of the room fall away to reveal the void beyond. It's as if this living room is a stage set in a vast theater of nothingness.

The Moons' house breaks apart like a three-dimensional painting on glass. I haul ass, weaving back and forth to dodge falling chunks of scenery and duck the whizzing razor shards thrown by the shattering pieces. Some sections hit the ground with so much force they bounce me into the air. Like a mouse fleeing from a diorama under a spotlight, I sprint into the infinity of darkness, the dining room shrinking into a pale grey box.

Way out here, nothing falls around me, but I keep running.

Didn't get an explosion of white this time. Something's changing, and I don't like the suggestion of what shattering pieces of falling debris imply. Taken by a powerful urge to get the hell out of here, I sprint in as straight a line as possible considering the total lack of anything around me. Only the sight of my body proves my eyes are still open.

Soft bumping noises somewhere in front of me, hands beating on a sliding glass door, give me a point of reference. I head toward the commotion. Dark grey walls appear far away, high up on either side. Three giant slabs of unknown matter hang in space around me, one above, one to either side. They stretch forward to infinity, gradually descending to enclose me in a featureless corridor.

I keep running.

A blur appears ahead of me… pale violet. At first it seems to be mist, but it solidifies into a faceted crystalline wall. Multiple people on the other side slap and pound at it, trying to break the lavender glass. I commit to a charge, lowering my left shoulder into a ramming posture.

The crystal wall emits a dull *crunch* when I hit it, the barrier giving in a crackling-squishy way like automotive glass on top of gym mats. Growling, I keep pushing forward, stretching the gooey substance. Flakes of violet crystal fall around me. Holes form. Hands reach in and grab me, pulling me forward, tearing apart the shining material.

Finally, the wall snaps, dumping me out on the floor on my chest upon a bed of crunching, thin crystal in a large cave of teal-colored stone. A bunch of women and one barefoot little girl in a dress surround me. I push myself upright, two of the women helping me stand.

Sams.

I'm literally beside myself.

Kid-Sam, 18-Sam, 37-Sam, HUD-Sam, and 24-Sam are all here, staring at me. Kid-Sam looks terrified. HUD-Sam has this 'well, you really screwed up, didn't you' expression. The others appear mildly freaked out.

I look left and right down the cave passage. Except for being the color of surgical scrubs, it appears reasonably normal. Behind me, a shallow alcove about the size of a phone booth emits a continuous stream of smoke. Ever see one of those space movies where people get in stasis pods for a long trip? Yeah, this looks like the medieval 'magic' version of one of those. Just a hole in the rock under a crystal hatch. Whoa. Azrael said my body stayed in one place while my soul went on to different worlds. Total *Matrix* situation, only via magic instead of a wire into my brain. That certainly explains why I couldn't teleport inside.

"We're not in Kansas anymore, are we?" I ask.

"Nope," says 37-Sam.

"We're not from Kansas. We're from California." Kid-Sam peers down at her bare feet, which are surrounded by sharp crystalline fragments.

Can't help it. I pick her up. Everyone else has shoes. They always say 'you have to help yourself before you can help others,' but this is taking things a bit too literally.

"Is this reality or another alternate dimension?" I ask.

"Alternate dimensions *are* reality." HUD-Sam smirks at me. "My Elizabeth says your Elizabeth is an idiot."

"And why's that?" I ask.

"She didn't destroy you." HUD-Sam folds her arms. "No idea why she bothered with this mess and dragged us all into it."

"This mess?" asks 24-Sam.

"Are you all idiots?" HUD-Sam sighs. "This is a dimensional soul prison. She created it in between actual dimensions to put you someplace where you couldn't interfere with her plans. Clearly, she underestimated your resolve. No doubt, she assumed you'd crack and get caught in an infinity loop of feeling sorry for yourself or some such drivel."

I step out of the crystal fragments and set Kid-Sam back on her feet. "Well, I'm not the frightened mouse I used to be."

24-Sam looks down, ashamed. She, of course, is still working through her issues.

"Snap out of it," says HUD-Sam to her. "We're

stronger than that."

"Why are you so pale?" asks Kid-Sam.

"She's a vampire in her dimension." 37-Sam shivers. "The bitch got Mary Lou in mine."

"Don't call her a bitch." HUD-Sam narrows her eyes.

I rub my forehead, trying to make sense of this. "Okay, so if this is a soul prison trying to trap me in-between dimensions, what are all of you doing here? Are you even real?"

"Yes." HUD-Sam brushes crystal dust from her blazer sleeves. "Your Elizabeth linked your consciousness to our dimensions to torment you. When you destroyed the links to each dimension and snapped back to this place, it somehow pulled us with you."

"Wouldn't it have made more sense for Elizabeth to stick me in an alternate dimension where I don't realize it's an alternate dimension rather than create these weird 'puzzles'?"

HUD-Sam laughs. "Yes, it would have been better to trap you in a reality you thought was your own. But she had to work with the materials available. Parallel dimensions containing you and your family in similar enough circumstances are not exactly commonplace. Samantha Moon only exists in .004 percent of realities. Same can be said for anyone, really. Many iterations of Earth exist where random chance produces different people. In most worlds, your ancestors from 2,000 generations back never met."

“My head hurts,” says 24-Sam.

“You should be used to it by now, dearie.” HUD-Sam fake smiles at her. “She is so demure it’s almost cute… if not for being utterly nauseating.”

A distant rumble rolls overhead.

Kid-Sam jumps and stares up at the cave ceiling. “I hate thunder.”

“Not thunder, sweetie.” HUD-Sam flashes a saccharin smile. “Magic of this magnitude is as delicate as a house of playing cards. Goody-Two-Shoes-Sam here broke her cell, so the whole Eternity Prison is going to fall apart.”

Dolores Brandt and her freakin’ obscure visions. I’d gone to see this tarot card reader fourteen years ago while trying to come to terms with what had happened to me vis-à-vis becoming a vampire. During our first session, she told me about some great metamorphosis I’d go through… which I now think refers to my separation from Elizabeth and becoming a psychic vampire instead of an undead. Back then, I thought she meant vampire in general. Though, I suppose it made little sense to speak of an already-happened event as if it hadn’t yet occurred. I’d gone back to visit her a few times, and on one such visit, she told me I’d end up in an eternity prison, but I took it the wrong way… thinking she meant vampire. Tarot predictions are aggravating, really. While they can be accurate, they’re often so vague as to only make sense in hindsight. Not terribly useful for avoiding bad situations when stuff only becomes clear after the fact. Wow. It’s been a while since I spoke to her. Wonder if she's still alive."She's not a goody two shoes," says 24-Sam. "And you're kinda bitchy."

"Yeah," mutters Kid-Sam.

"Agreed." 37-Sam gestures at me. "She's normal. But you're kinda dark. But it's okay. We know it's Elizabeth's influence."

"Whatever." HUD-Sam glares down the cave. "If we don't want to be destroyed along with this place when it collapses, we need to all go back to our realities."

"Great idea," I say. "But how?"

"This place should not exist." HUD-Sam examines her pointy fingernails. "Your Elizabeth created it. It is most likely arranged like a Lichtenberg figure. We merely have to find the origin point, or root, where reality bends into a portal."

"Can you say that again but in English?" asks 24-Sam.

HUD-Sam grumbles.

"Let me…" I gaze around at the cave. "Basically, HUD-Sam is saying these caves are shaped like frozen lightning and all the branching passages converge on a central point."

"Okay, sounds easy enough." 37-Sam starts walking to the left. "How do we tell which way to go?"

"I'd imagine the cave will get thinner if we're going the wrong way."

We all follow her.

"How much time do we have?" asks 24-Sam,

sliding next to me.

"It's difficult to predict," says HUD-Sam. "My Elizabeth cannot wield magic of this scope in her present form. However, I suspect each cell we breach will hasten the complete destruction of this quasi-plane exponentially. The safest way out for us would be to leave everyone else in their cells… but I know the rest of you lack the stomach for that."

"Oh, come on." I shoot her a look. "Even *you* wouldn't leave Tammy and Anthony behind."

I get major side eye back, but she doesn't argue.

"This place is really freaky," says Kid-Sam. "I wanna go home."

"Same here, Kid-Me." I exhale. "Same here."

It occurs to me teleportation will likely work again since I'm no longer trapped in magical sleep while my consciousness floats around alternate dimensions. Could explain why I seemed ghostly there, since I'd basically gone astrally wandering rather than physically jumping from dimension to dimension. Major problem being, my teleportation ability can't go between dimensions. To the Moon, Mars, hell, other galaxies probably… but all of those places are still inside my dimensional world. Dimensions are, after all, pretty big. Almost as big as a CVS receipt. Maybe not technically being in any dimension at the moment would allow me to teleport into one, but it also might cause me to explode. If there's a doorway out, we're better off taking it.

Besides, I need to find my kids, Allie, Kingsley,

and whoever else is trapped in here.

We group of Sams jog down the hallway, mostly silent except for the click of HUD-Sam's high heels and the patter of Kid-Sam's bare feet on the stone. It's weird seeing doubt on evil-me's face. Equally weird is 24-Sam showing some fierceness. Kid-Sam appears to be seriously homesick, which is also surprising. At her age, I'd have missed Mary Lou more than my 'home.' 37-Sam seems calmer, less frazzled. Maybe she and Rick will get together after all.

"Stupid question," I say. "If I really visited your realities, even as a projection, is anything going to change for you based on meeting me? Or was everything—*is* everything—happening here all inside my head?"

The multi-Sams discuss their respective lives briefly as we jog along, and come to the conclusion that, yes, changes will happen. Kid-Sam will stifle her destructive impulses and cling to Mary Lou for help. 24-Sam might accelerate the timetable on asking Danny to defend her, but not push *too* hard. 37-Sam sounds interested in potentially remarrying—with Rick—combining our families. HUD-Sam says she's 'open to the idea' of giving up on the job and using her mind powers to amass a comfortable fortune. She complains a little about Anthony, permanently seven years old due to being a vampire, acting a bit spoiled lately. 37-Sam breaks down, kinda yelling at her for being ungrateful since her Anthony died. She'd tolerate any amount of brattiness to have him back.

"Oh, he's not bratty. Merely a bit spoiled," says HUD-Sam.

I don't comment on her Tammy being scared shitless of her. Despite what HUD-Sam says, I'm certain her Tammy is psychic, too, and knows exactly how dark her mother's gotten. Those photos on her desk told a sad story. HUD-Sam is exactly what Danny feared me turning into.

"I promise not to blow anyone up," says Kid-Sam.

"Good." I overact a sigh of relief. "Oh, one thing…"

She peers up at me.

"Don't let anyone tell you faeries aren't real."

Kid-Sam starts to blush, but gawks instead. "I didn't imagine her?"

"Nope. Embrace it. We come from a long line of nature witches. The faeries are sniffing you out. Talk to them. Don't be like me. I let Mary Lou convince me faeries are nonsense for little kids."

"They are," says HUD-Sam.

I point at her. "See? Don't listen to her. Spend too long in a government job, you end up as a pale, fanged ghoul incapable of joy."

HUD-Sam is unimpressed.

24-Sam laughs. "Gee, maybe I should change careers now."

"I was mostly making a joke… but as soon as it stops being a source of happiness, yeah. Definitely leave. Think about private investigations."

"I'm gonna grow up to be a famous international jewel-thief and live on trains with the hobos," says Kid-Sam.

The other Sams all chuckle.

Yeah, I really did have that 'dream' for about four months before I forgot it and moved on to wanting to be a girl version of Indiana Jones.

"Since you are all a bunch of bleeding-hearts," says HUD-Sam, "keep an eye out for crystal tombs. Anyone still inside one when this place collapses will be lost."

"Do you have any idea how many are trapped here?"

"Only a dozen or so… plus everyone you love."

Grr.

"How do we find them?" I growl.

"Unless you can steal thoughts from your Elizabeth's mind, our only option is the simplistic and most time consuming one. We run around looking." HUD-Sam points ahead. "Which is why I suggest we simply leave. The others will reincarnate someday. Though, if you want to stop for the kids, breaking two crystals won't speed up the collapse *too* much."

Yeah, right. Not happening. The kids are definitely getting busted out. But I can't leave anyone here on purpose—especially Allison or Kingsley.

Chapter Eighteen
Mourn Later, Run Now

The cave is a pain in the ass to run through.

It jags up and down, left and right, pretty much exactly like we're inside a lightning bolt—only with *much* less electricity. Here, it's about the width of a subway tube, and impossible to tell if it's getting smaller or not. I don't know if we're running toward or away from the base.

Purple light up ahead breaks the monotony of the surrounding darkness. It looks like the glowing lid of a coffin standing upright, like something Sleeping Beauty might have been stuck inside. The crystalline shell is eight feet tall and slightly wider than a standard house door. The chamber behind it is about the size of a shower stall. Inside, Ramani Koor—one of the kidnapped creators—floats as if in liquid, her hair drifting upward slightly. Magic has to be levitating her rather than fluid, or I'd be soaked.

Okay, guess I figured out what Elizabeth did with the creators. Since this woman wasn't in Venezuela, it stands to reason Liz made the Eternity Prison a while ago, intending to stick the creators here forever so they could keep her reality working.

I do the only thing I can think of and withdraw the Devil Killer. I tell the others to stand back, and, holding the weapon in both hands, slash the shimmering cage a good foot or so above the top of her head to avoid accidentally clipping her. The instant my sword strikes the crystal, the whole thing shatters into pieces so damn small it's more of a powder. An answering thunderclap shakes the cave, as if this reality is reacting to me breaking a cell open.

"Told you," says HUD-Sam.

37-Sam picks Kid-Sam up so she doesn't step on broken glass.

Ramani floats down to her feet and opens her eyes. She starts to scream in shock, but calms in a second or two, hand pressed over her heart. "Sam?" The woman peers past me. "And… Sam? And… what the heck?"

"We were trapped in alternate dimensions," I say.

"How did you escape? I kept repeating the same frustrating day over and over."

"No time to explain. We have to get out of here."

Another, quieter rumble crackles overhead.

"Time to go!" yells 24-Sam. "Come on."

We run down the cave, still having no idea which way we're going. Finding even one branching passage would tell me which way goes to the exit, but thus far, the tunnel has been mostly solid. Upon spotting another crystal container coming up on the right, I slow for a peek… but it's empty. No point smashing it. Not far past it, we finally reach a branching passage, and it's heading back the way we came from.

Good sign. Means we've been running toward the exit.

Except… something makes me want to go in this new direction.

When a psychic gets a hunch, they should listen to it.

The multi-Sams stand there yelling at me that I'm going the wrong way.

"I know! I'm feeling a pull or something."

Grumbling, they follow me down the new tunnel. Voices up ahead pull me to a sprint. Sounds like Anthony and small child talking about which way to go.

"Ant!" I yell.

"Here!" shouts Anthony, along with a strangely familiar child's voice.

The cave floor jags upward at a steep angle, forcing me to sprout my wings and fly-leap to get past it. I land at the top of a twelve-foot nearly vertical shaft, stunned to find two Anthonys running toward me. One looks like I expect—a tall young man—only he's wearing teal medical scrubs. The other one's seven years old and in a hospital gown.

Seeing my son little again is too much for me. I can't resist scooping him up and squeezing him. Ack! He's got no body temperature. I still cling to him, but give big-Anthony a 'what happened' stare.

"Ma!" He runs in, grabs me, and breaks down crying.

Dammit. Dammit. Dammit. Something is severely wrong.

He might be taller than me, but I am still an immortal. I pick both of my sons up, turn, and 'ski' down the steep floor using my wings as a parachute. As soon as we reach the bottom, big-Anthony picks *me* up, damn near crushing me against his chest in a hug.

37-Sam takes one look at kid-Anthony in a hospital gown and sobs. In her reality, she lost him. The sight of him in the gown he died in is way too much for her to process.

I hand child-Anthony to her. "Here. He's fine."

She grabs him like a giant doll, repeating, "My baby!" in an endless loop.

"Ant?" I ask. "What's wrong?"

He keeps crying.

"Clock's ticking," says HUD-Sam.

"Ma..." Anthony clears his throat, sets me down, and forces himself to stop crying. "It's Dad. Elizabeth sent us to an alternate dimension. A hospital where I was about to die as a little kid. Dad saved him. He's... gone." Ant rushes an explanation of Danny flowing out of him into child Anthony, turning him into a vampire sorta like I did… only without an amulet on hand to reverse it.

Normally, any mention of Danny puts me in a bad mood. But I bite the negativity back for Anthony's sake.

"I'm a vampire now," says little-Anthony. "That's awesome! My fangs don't work yet, though."

"Wait…" HUD-Sam points at him. "How did Danny do this?"

"Remember me telling you how he dabbled in blood magic? He kinda turned into a half-assed dark master," I say.

"Danny? A dark master? Possessing our son?" HUD-Sam blinks, blinks again, then laughs so hard she can't speak another word.

Not sure what about the situation is funny. Hopefully, she's mocking Danny for being a dark master.

"How did he follow you out?" I point to little-Ant.

Anthony shrugs. "Probably the same way all these versions of you are here." He chuckles, pointing to Kid-Sam. "By the way, Ma, you were adorable as a kid."

Kid-Sam smiles cheesily as if to say 'I know!'

37-Sam continues squeezing baby Anthony, sobbing. Good grief. It's going to take a pound of C4 to separate them so they can go back to their respective realities. Whatever. I can worry about it later. We have to get going.

I touch my son's face. Wow, he might actually need a shave. "Azrael was right… you made it out."

"He's here?" asks Anthony.

"Briefly popped in, yeah."

Anthony looks back at the angled wall behind us. "Where's Tammy?"

"Not sure yet, I… Hang on. Everyone give me a moment of quiet."

Reality shakes as another thunderclap rolls.

"That goes for you too, fake world," I grumble.

After a moment of trying to open myself up to gut feelings, a definite pull draws me back out into the original tunnel we started in. Even better, it's pulling me in the same direction we'd been going all along.

"This way!" I yell, before running.

Chapter Nineteen
Crumbling

Since I don't need any help breaking down the crystal prisons—and there's no way to lose the others in a straight cave—I jump up onto my wings.

Flying at about 120 miles per hour is way faster than I can run, even with vampiric speed. HUD-Sam is pretty damn fast, though. She's taken her high heels off and appears to be doing about sixty-five MPH on foot.

I reach another crystal prison. The vague form inside is so damn big it can only be one person. I smash it open, triggering another minor earthquake and accompanying thunder. The big guy springs out of the chamber, punching at a nonexistent adversary. Being shorter and faster than him, it's easy for me to get out of the way.

Kingsley swings so hard he takes himself off his feet and lands in a heap.

24-Sam covers Kid-Sam's eyes.

Vampire-Anthony thinks naked Kingsley is hilarious and starts laughing. The rest of the Sams ogle him in varying degrees of subtlety, except for 37-Sam who's too wrapped up in holding her little boy again to even notice the big guy in his full Greek god glory.

"Need a minute, Sam," says Kingsley, his voice more growl than human. "So… damn… angry."

I back off. "I'd say take your time, but we don't have any."

He stands, glaring around—until he notices the crowd behind me. "Having an identity crisis?"

"Close. A multiple realities crisis."

"Figured. Got stuck in one myself. So damn frustrating."

Yeah, pretty obvious he couldn't escape his trap. I'm guessing because it played on his anger issues. Can't hold it against him really since he's a werewolf. Anger is kinda their thing. I pat him on the shoulder, then explain this whole place is going to deconstruct itself soon and kill us all, so we have to get out.

As there is nothing here for him to wear and no Allison to make an illusion for him (my magic isn't strong enough to create illusions for others), he shifts to wolf form. I take off again, racing down the jagged lightning-shaped cave. This passage appears to be a main shaft, so it's not as bad in terms of sudden hard-to-climb walls or pitfalls.

A few minutes past Kingsley's chamber, I spot

another crystal door and it's screaming at me. Not verbally screaming... rather, emotional radiance. I rush a little too much to get there and have a mild issue with braking. After bouncing face-first off the crystal, I land on my feet and peer in at Tammy. She *looks* fine, but something is very, very wrong.

"Tam!" I shout, stabbing the Devil Killer into the barrier.

The crystalline wall explodes in a shower of purple dust. Tammy gracefully floats down to her feet, then collapses on the floor, curling into a ball. She grabs her stomach, apparently unconscious.

I drop to my knees, forcing myself not to panic, and check her over for injuries. "Tam?"

"Mommy?" whispers Tammy. "Help…"

"I'm here. What's wrong, baby?"

Her eyes flutter open. She looks up at me with a face she hasn't made since she was tiny… the same look she had on after waking from nightmares. The fear in her eyes lasts only a few seconds before she gazes around at the cave.

Wincing, she pulls her T-shirt up to examine her stomach, but appears surprised for some reason.

"Oh… whew…" She drops her shirt back into place and goes limp, head in my lap.

I raise an eyebrow. "What's wrong? You look fine."

"Nothing. Crazy bitch stabbed me. Wasn't real. Just a dream."

"It was more real than dream," I say.

"Can't be… or I'd be dying." She pushes herself

up to sit and grabs me in a hug.

"Alternate dimensions, astral projection. Your body wasn't really there, but the place you went to really exists."

Tammy whimpers something I can't make out and squeezes me tighter. "I'm sorry."

"You didn't do anything wrong."

"No, I mean… for being a bitch to you a couple years ago. Thank you for always being there for me." She sniffles.

Anthony jogs up to us. "You okay, Tam?"

She wipes her nose. "I don't know. Gawd, I am such a failure."

"No you're not," I say.

"Not me, the other Tammy. In there."

"What happened?" I ask.

"Remember when I was four and you got shot?"

"Yeah. How could I forget? I think I still have a bruise from that." I wink. "Feel it every time it rains." I don't, but every old cop says that.

"In that place, you didn't have a vest on and died. I turned into such a crazy, selfish self-destructive little bitch."

I pull her to her feet. "Can you hold it together for a little bit? We have to get out of here fast or we're all going to die. We can talk all you want once we're not about to be lost to eternity."

"What's going...?" In a matter of seconds, she's read the situation out of my thoughts. It's enough to scare her calm. "Oh wow…" She looks at Anthony for a few seconds. "Holy crap… Dad's gone?" She covers her mouth. "Why am I even sad? He was such a jerk to Mom."

"Oh, I almost forgot," says Anthony. "Ma, Dad wanted me to tell you he's sorry for not believing you when you said, 'I'm still me.'"

In an instant, my memory leaps back to that night thirteen years ago, me standing there in our house, practically begging Danny to believe I hadn't been replaced by some monster. I stood there, whispering 'I'm still me' to myself a few times after he stormed off, leaving me there, feeling like a disgusting creature.

I should hate Danny for doing that to me, but hearing him apologize—more than a bit too late—nearly brings me to the verge of tears.

Anthony snaps his fingers. "*That's* why Mini-Me is here. Dad's soul is his dark master. Dad belongs to our dimension, so he popped out with me."

"Wait, so does baby Anthony belong to our dimension or the dimension you took him from?" I ask. "Am I going to have two of you? Hope it doesn't mess with, you know, the fabric of the universe. Whatever that is."

37-Sam twists away, clinging defensively to baby-Anthony. Uh oh. I don't think she's going to give him up. Not only is she inconsolable over losing him, her version of Tammy was ready to kill herself to see her brother again. If she keeps him, she's probably thinking she might save both of them.

She wants him pretty bad, Mom, says Tammy in my head. *She's legit going to try to kill anyone who attempts to stop her from bringing him home.*

Argh. Do we technically 'belong' to our dimensions or can we go anywhere?

"No idea, Mom," says Tammy, "but we better go somewhere fast."

I look at my daughter. She points up at a huge section of cave ceiling peeling away and flying off into a starscape. For a second, I'm paralyzed by terror, kinda like being in a spaceship and watching the hull open up directly to outer space when I don't have a suit on. Only, no powerful vacuum force sucks us out into the empty void.

"Mom!" yells Tammy.

Right.

A powerful earthquake throws us all to the ground. Multiple crashes follow in sequence, so loud they hurt my brain.

"We need to get out of here, now!" says Anthony.

Without missing a beat, Kid-Sam jumps onto Kingsley's back like he's a giant furry horse, grinning from ear to ear, having the time of her life. The big guy doesn't seem to mind, giving her just enough time to get a good fistful of hair before he bolts off. Works for me… he can run much faster than a little kid.

"Go!" I shout. "Follow that wolf!"

Chapter Twenty
Headcanon

Our tunnel finally merges into a larger branching passage.

We run downhill to the left, avoiding a secondary jag that goes deeper into the eternity prison. No weird hunches pull me toward it, so I keep going in the direction of the 'lighting tree root.'

"We still have to find Allison. Can you locate her, Tam?"

"Oh, duh!" Tammy pulls her faerie amulet off and stuffs it in her pocket. After a few seconds, she points behind us.

We reverse up the main passage, doing the exact opposite of what people should do when trapped inside a fast-disintegrating alternate reality—go deeper into the damn place. Chunks of teal stone fall from the ceiling, some crashing into the ground beside or behind us, others hovering in place for a moment before rocketing out into space.

The next crystal we find contains the creator, Quentin Arnbury. I smash the barrier. He staggers out of the cell, white-faced as if terrified, but rapidly composes himself.

"Where are we?"

"A sort of soul prison," I say. "But it's disintegrating. We have to go."

He nods.

Tammy points ahead. "Allison's this way."

Forty feet down the same passage, we pause to break open another crystal, releasing the next creator, Lance Blackburn. He looks disappointed, then confused at being in a cave. Leaving him to the Multi-Sams for explanations, I rush ahead with Tammy.

Cracks start splitting the floor under us, but they're relatively easy to jump over.

A frustratingly long run down a narrow branch later, Tammy drags me by the hand up to Allison's chamber. I give it a good whack from the Devil Killer, shattering the barrier. My sword striking the crystal wall resonates over the entire eternity prison. I feel like a hamster in a cardboard box someone walloped with a baseball bat.

Once again, the quake knocks everyone to the ground—except Allison, who hovers inside the chamber. She sinks to her feet, her hair settling around her.

"… throw your life away in this strip club!" shouts Allison, pointing at me.

"Um, I think you have me confused with someone else," I say.

Allison goes scarlet in the face. "Holy crap! That was so real!"

Our mental link reconnects. In a matter of a second or two, I see her trapped in an alternate reality where she's trying to talk a version of herself away from a life of being a stripper/prostitute. Needless to say, she didn't have much luck.

"She wouldn't listen to me!" yells Allison. "Am I really that frustrating to argue with, Sam?"

"Of course not. We were thrown into soul traps designed specifically to attack our most vulnerable fears, weaknesses, and bad memories… or something."

"What's a strip club?" asks baby-Anthony. "Daddy won't explain it."

"Guilty conscience," grumbles Tammy.

Allison looks at little Anthony and squeals. "Oh my God! He's adorable!"

37-Sam squeezes him as if afraid Allie is going to try and swipe the boy from her arms.

"What's going on?" asks Allison, eyeing the crowd around us.

"No time!" yells just about everyone at once.

We run in a group back to the main passage, weaving around falling chunks of ceiling, jumping gaps in the floor, and dodging random floating fragments hanging in the middle of the cave neither falling nor shooting off. So weird.

Kid-Sam rides Kingsley like a horse, cheering

and loving every minute of it, likely unaware of the danger we're all in. This passage merges into another, even bigger, passage after about 200 yards.

"We have to be getting close to the gate," yells Anthony.

The cave jags upward at a sharp angle, but it's only a five-foot-high problem. Even Lance Blackburn can get over it unassisted. Past the bump, the cave widens even more. Over the course of about a hundred yards, it becomes so vast a 747 could fly around in here. Wait… it's not a cave, but a huge bowl-shaped crater a few miles across. In defiance of gravity, we run-float out of the passage behind us, gliding to an enormous hovering crystal island. The platform is ice rink smooth, surrounded by regularly spaced rock pillars. Most are plain rock, but several of them have swirling portals of red energy hovering in front of them.

"We made it!" yells Tammy.

"Not for you, no." HUD-Sam points around at the portals. "These connect to *our* various dimensions… but this eternity prison was created from yours. To return to the world you belong in, you need to find the primary portal."

"Which is where?" I ask.

HUD-Sam points past the island into the star field. "Keep going that way. It looks like outer space but it isn't. This area is still inside the eternity prison."

"Why is that one orange and all the others red?" asks 24-Sam.

"Because it's yours. Only you see it as orange." HUD-Sam looks at me as if to say 'she is such a ditz' before walking into a swirling red portal... and disappearing.

18-Sam exhales. "Hey, thanks for what you did. Guess I gotta get my life sorted out and stuff."

"You're welcome." I hug her. "Do what you feel is right for you, and don't let our curmudgeon of a father tell you what you can or can't dream about."

"I won't," says 18-Sam. "Gee, I hope I don't get turned into a vampire. Wish I knew if it would happen or not so I don't bust my ass in college for no reason."

"Ha. College isn't right for everyone. But I think it was for me. Up to you. But you know how our luck is. If you *don't* go, you probably won't turn into a vampire, and then you'll kick yourself."

"Hah. Yeah, probably." 18-Sam grins, then sprints across the island to a portal.

24-Sam smiles brightly, waves goodbye, and dashes into another portal. Kid-Sam points one out as orange to her. Kingsley trots over to it. She slides down from him, gives him a big hug, and runs into the swirl. Baby Anthony looks at a portal on the right side as 37-Sam carries him in the opposite direction to a different gateway. He glances back and forth between what must be 'his' portal and her, then rests his head on her shoulder, seemingly content.

"Wait!" I shout.

37-Sam runs faster.

Quentin smiles. "It's okay. She needs him, too."

Clingy-Sam skids to a stop by her portal, peering back at us with a 'seriously? You're not pissed at me?' expression.

I turn to Quentin, confused as well. "Did you do something?"

Quentin clears his throat. "The portals between dimensions somehow split the boy, creating two copies of him. One who remains with his family in his dimension, another who came with his older self to this soul prison."

"He... he can come home with me?" asks 37-Sam, shocked.

"I don't think it works that way," says Lance.

"It does now," says Quentin. "Meaning, as soon as I decided that's what happened, it became reality. I'll write it down once I'm home." He taps his head. "For now, it's pretty clear up here."

"Wait, aren't you the guy who kills twenty characters per book for fun?" asks Ramani. "You're like the last person I'd think would write a 'feel good' ending."

"I… well…" Quentin coughs.

"He got stuck in his fictional world of Estaeron," says Tammy. "The people of the dimension recognized him as a fallen god responsible for all the killing and stuff. He was repeatedly convicted of murder and other crimes. They executed him over and over again."

Quentin pales. "Yes, well, perhaps there is such

a thing as killing off *too* many characters. Besides, look how happy they are together. That woman would kill to protect that boy."

"Damn right she would." I pat my Anthony on the shoulder, then nod at 37-Sam.

37-Sam bows gratefully, then darts into her portal, carrying vampire child-Anthony.

"Their life's about to get seriously weird," says Anthony.

"No weirder than ours… and her Tammy *really* needs her brother back." I squeeze Tammy's hand.

A massive crash shakes the world. Everyone still on the island platform spins around at the same time to look at the enormous cave behind us belching a geyser of glimmering crystal fragments, the shattered remains of more delicate passages collapsing in on themselves. We're about to learn what it's like to be downwind of a razor blade factory in the middle of a tornado.

"Mr. Arnbury," says Tammy. "Can you create a spaceship or something?"

"Alas, it doesn't work that way, kid. I cannot alter the reality I am presently occupying."

"Then everyone run!" yells Allison.

"I'd like to point that we're stuck on a floating island," says Ramani.

"We ran across air to get here, didn't we?" Anthony starts sprinting directly away from the storm of crystal razors.

"He has a point," I yell, following.

A few fast-moving razor shards zip by my head.

Anthony hurls himself off the far end of the island, somehow managing to keep 'running' forward without falling. A horrendous *crack* comes from behind me. The island buckles inward, flipping us up into the air. The barrage of crystal daggers strikes the floundering island, further breaking the glass-like slab into smaller and smaller pieces—but it effectively stops the projectiles from shredding us.

"There!" yells Allison, pointing. "Directly opposite the big cave. That white spot!"

I extend my wings and zip around, collecting everyone in this weightless non-space.

One by one, I grab Tammy, Anthony, Allison, Kingsley, Quentin, Lance, and Ramani, throwing them in the direction she pointed. It's like I'm wrangling astronauts in zero-g.

Hope this doorway leads home.

Arms at my sides, I lean into a dive for the giant white portal...

Chapter Twenty-one
Final Boss

My aim was mostly on point.

I need to chase and adjust a few times to keep everyone cruising on course as we glide across a vast expanse of open nothingness toward a swirling white portal. Behind us, the jagged arms of the soul prison's corridors extend into the star field, a snap-shot of a massive multi-branched lightning strike. From here, the individual caves seem tiny and delicate. They collapse inward, following the pull of gravity aligned to the center of the structure. It's beyond surreal to witness.

Tammy's the first to reach the swirl and disap-pear. Ramani follows seconds later. The portal is so damn wide there's no way anyone's going to miss now, so I dash ahead and dive in. Feels like I've done a face-plant into electrified cotton candy. The cobweb-breaking sensation lasts only an instant before I'm on my feet, again standing on a mirror-like crystalline surface in another huge cave.

Tammy and Ramani stare transfixed at an enormous black demon-dragon sitting catlike in front of a far more modest swirling orange portal. The creature is probably about 250 feet long from nose to tail, partially skeletal, and yeah… it's the exact same bastard I faced in Talos's world. Considering I stabbed it in the heart with the Devil Killer, no way is this thing real. If it is, it's some other demon who looks the same.

"Oh, what the hell is he doing here?" I ask.

My daughter stares at me in shock for being so blasé.

"Final boss," says Anthony, referring to the bad guys in video games. "Gotta beat him to get to the portal."

The ground bucks and shakes under us. Splintering cracks race across the star field above us, making it look like a movie screen made of glass.

I stuff the Devil Killer back in its sheath, then hold my hands out to either side. "We don't have time for this."

My kids know the drill already. Each takes my hand. Tammy grabs Allison, who grabs Ramani's hand. Anthony takes Quentin's hand.

Lance shrugs and grips Quentin's other hand. "I'm guessing you aren't planning to start singing Kumbaya?"

I focus on the portal behind the dragon and call the dancing flame. A small version of this room appears inside the orange glow, rapidly growing as it rushes toward me. In an instant, the fire curtain blows past us and we're standing by the portal, right behind the demon dragon.

It roars at our sudden disappearance, lurching to its feet. The damn thing's so huge it shakes the ground by simply moving. Great slabs of star-field-covered matter fall from the dome overhead, walloping the dragon over the head, breaking across its left wing, and ripping a hole in its side.

A wave of disintegration rolls across the floor, racing toward us.

"Go!" I yell, shoving my kids at the orange swirl.

The dragon falls off the ledge as the floor vanishes out from under it.

Ramani and Quentin jump through. I grab Lance and shove him into the portal. Allison and Kingsley dive in. The floor vanishes out from under my feet as I jump toward the blinding orange glow.

The roaring falls silent.

Chapter Twenty-two
Dark Masters are Forever

I slap into the ground on my chest, wings at a weird angle. The dirt tastes scorched.

I push myself upright, surprised to find us at the approximate center of a hundred-yard-wide burn patch where all the vegetation has evaporated. Behind us, one face of the large ziggurat stands exposed to the air—all the vines and such burned away.

Nearby, Anthony chuckles.

"Why are you laughing?" I ask.

"You kinda looked like a bird after it flew into a window."

Tammy swats him.

Okay, that's funny. I laugh, too—at least until I gaze around at the Venezuelan jungle at the edge of the burn patch. I'm pretty sure we're in the same place as before, only there's no sign of Elizabeth, ascendant dark masters, or anyone else here. It's eerily quiet.

Tammy grabs my arm. "Mom…"

"We're okay." I pull her in, hold her close.

"The other Tammy wasn't real, was she?"

"In the other dimension, she was."

Tammy sniffles. "Am I really like that?"

Before I can think 'like what?' she floods my head with her memories of her alternate reality. Oh, wow. I am *so* damn grateful she didn't see younger Tammy's head hit the back end of that truck. Which means I don't see it, either. Wow, merely the thought of it happening drives me to tears and gets me squeezing her tighter, grateful she's here and alive.

It's okay, Mom. Quentin's gonna help her.

Huh, what?

I begged him to do something 'cause I was too much of a screw up to stop her from getting killed. He's gonna write that you actually got turned into a vampire and faked being shot on the job. Meaning, she will have a mom now. Young me's gonna mellow out with you there. She sniffles into my shoulder. *Like how you kept me from going too dark.*

I hate the thought my daughter might really have gone off the deep end if I'd died during that drug raid all those years ago.

You weren't half as bratty as you think you were.

She cry-laughs. *Trust me, I see that now.* Her emotions pause. *Oh my God... you caught me trying to hang myself at ten?*

I cringe, then sigh. Yes, but not every alternate reality is a good replica of us. That Tammy was an exaggeration.

Okay. But you and Uncle Rick though? Ick.

I laugh. Hey, tragedy makes for unlikely matches.

Anthony wanders off to the edge of the scorched earth, gazing into the jungle. Tammy glances toward him. She doesn't have to tell me he's having a difficult time dealing with Danny leaving him. I can see it.

We walk over to him.

"Hey, kiddo," I say in a soft voice.

"Hey, ma…"

"Hey, dork." Tammy threads her arm around his. "You okay?"

"I suppose. I just miss him."

I stand beside him, letting him grieve, contemplate, and try to come to terms with having his head all to himself again. Kingsley runs off into the jungle in search of his clothes. Allison paces around the middle of the circular burn area, examining the ground. The three creators gather in a group, discussing where they are, how they're going to return home, and if Elizabeth will come after them again.

"He had to do it," says Anthony. "Dad's been acting weird for months."

"He's been weird a lot longer than that," mutters Tammy.

Anthony shakes his head. "No, I mean like… it

felt as if he wanted to leave for a while. He really didn't *want* to go away, but he told me my path is going somewhere he can't follow. Any idea what that means?"

"Probably doesn't wanna watch you on your dates," says Tammy, elbowing him.

Anthony sighs. "No. He meant something bigger."

I stand between the kids, an arm around their shoulders. "Whatever it is, we'll get through it."

"Ma?"

"Yeah?"

"You did the right thing when you saved me. Not sure if you've ever wondered, but I'm glad you did it," says Anthony.

I exhale. Truth is, I've asked myself if I did the right thing almost daily since. "I've wondered if it was selfish of me to keep you here instead of letting your soul go off to seek its destiny."

"This *is* my destiny, I think." He smiles.

"What makes you say that?" asks Tammy.

"I dunno. Just a feeling. Like everything's the way it's supposed to be." He takes in some air. "Gonna miss Dad though."

"For what it's worth," says Kingsley, walking up behind us once again dressed in his own clothing, "Dark masters are forever."

Tammy rolls her eyes. "They're not diamonds."

Kingsley pats Anthony on the shoulder. "Danny's still out there. It's extremely difficult to destroy them."

"Well, what now?" asks Allison. "This place is a complete parking lot now."

"Any idea where the bitch went?" Anthony flicks at a partially burnt leaf.

"Language," I say.

"Sorry, ma."

Allison flaps her arms in a helpless sort of shrug. "Obviously, Elizabeth and company made a major portal here. Whatever happened, the amount of energy released melted those stone columns. Pretty sure they crossed over into another dimension."

"Also, obviously, the portal is closed," adds Kingsley.

"Can you reopen it?" I ask Allison.

"Uhh." Allison cringes. "Are you sure you want to? I mean, Elizabeth is gone from our world. She's not really our problem now."

"Yeah, she is. If you had a crazy dog and it got away from your house and started biting people, no one would say it's not your problem because he got out of the house." I kick at the still-smoking stone on the ground. "If it's impossible for us to find her, okay, fine. We tried. But if I can stop her from destroying an entire other world, I have to."

Anthony straightens up, puffing out his chest. "Yeah. We have to help."

"Dork," mutters Tammy, smiling.

He grins.

Allison scratches her head, staring at the ground. "Interdimensional portals are a little over my head, guys. I *might* be able to figure out where they went, but I don't understand the complexities of interdimensional navigation. That's like *really* heavy math and I kinda suck at it."

"So we have no way to go after her?" asks Kingsley, sounding relieved.

A glowing golden rectangle about the size of a door stretches open beside us. Max steps out of it, finger in the air. "I believe I can help."

The End

To be continued in:

Vampire Empress

Vampire for Hire #21

Coming soon!

About J.R. Rain:

J.R. Rain is an ex-private investigator who now writes full-time. He lives in a small house on a small island with his small dog, Sadie. Please visit him at www.jrrain.com.

About Matthew S. Cox:

Originally from South Amboy NJ, **Matthew S. Cox** has been creating science fiction and fantasy worlds for most of his reasoning life. Since 1996, he has developed the "Divergent Fates" world, in which Division Zero, Virtual Immortality, The Awakened Series, The Harmony Paradox, and the Daughter of Mars series take place.

Matthew is an avid gamer, a recovered WoW addict, Gamemaster for two custom systems, and a fan of anime, British humour, and intellectual science fiction that questions the nature of reality, life, and what happens after it.

He is also fond of cats.

Please find him at: www.matthewcoxbooks.com

Made in the USA
Las Vegas, NV
31 January 2021